Andrey Kurkov

DEATH AND THE PENGUIN

TRANSLATED FROM THE RUSSIAN BY
George Bird

VINTAGE

Published by Vintage 2003

2 4 6 8 10 9 7 5 3 1

Copyright © Andrey Kurkov 1996
Copyright © Diogenes Verlag AG, Zurich 1999
All rights but the Russian and Ukrainian reserved
English translation © George Bird 2001

Andrey Kurkov has asserted his right under the Copyright,
Designs and Patents Act, 1988 to be identified as the author
of this work

This book is sold subject to the condition that it shall not by
way of trade or otherwise, be lent, resold, hired out, or
otherwise circulated without the publisher's prior consent in
any form of binding or cover other than that in which it is
published and without a similar condition including this
condition being imposed on the subsequent purchaser

First published in 1996 with the title
Smert'postoronnego by the
Alterpress, Kiev

This translation was first published in 2001 by
The Harvill Press

Vintage
Random House, 20 Vauxhall Bridge Road,
London SW1V 2SA

Random House Australia (Pty) Limited
20 Alfred Street, Milsons Point, Sydney
New South Wales 2061, Australia

Random House New Zealand Limited
18 Poland Road, Glenfield,
Auckland 10, New Zealand

Random House (Pty) Limited
Endulini, 5A Jubilee Road, Parktown 2193,
South Africa

The Random House Group Limited Reg. No. 954009
www.randomhouse.co.uk

A CIP catalogue record for this book
is available from the British Library

ISBN 1 86046 945 0

Papers used by Random House are natural, recyclable
products made from wood grown in sustainable forests.
The manufacturing processes conform to the environ-
mental regulations of the country of origin

Printed and bound in Great Britain by
Bookmarque Ltd, Croydon, Surrey

'A brilliant satirical take on life in modern-day Kiev. Watch out, though, as Kurkov's writing style is addictive'
Punch

'Darkly comical thrillers are what we look forward to from the writers of the former USSR, and Ukrainian Kurkov conjures up both Gogol and Dostoevsky in a conspiracy laden plot...Genuinely original'
Scotsman

'Wistful but (thankfully) not whimsical. Funny, alarming, and, in a Slavic way, not unlike early Pinter'
Kirkus Reviews

'For all the air of menace, Kurkov keeps the tone light and the pace brisk in this marvellously entertaining and yet sobering work'
Age, Melbourne

'An original and sinister satire of chaotic, post-Soviet Ukraine...moving, thrilling and intelligent'
What's On

Kurkov's novel exists in an all-encompassing vacuum that, like a kind of narrative narcotic, insinuates itself into the reader's pores until what was once surreal has achieved its own normality...Kurkov is a strangely entrancing writer'
Booklist

'A successfully brooding novel, which creates an enduring sense of dismay and strangeness'
Times Literary Supplement

FOR THE SHARPS,
IN GRATITUDE

A Militia major is driving along when he sees a militiaman standing with a penguin.

"Take him to the zoo," he orders.

Some time later the same major is driving along when he sees the militiaman still with the penguin.

"What have you been doing?" he asks. "I said take him to the zoo."

"We've been to the zoo, Comrade Major," says the militiaman, "and the circus. And now we're going to the pictures."

CHARACTERS IN THE STORY

Viktor Alekseyevich Zolotaryov	a writer
Misha	his penguin
Igor Lvovich, the Chief	an editor
Sergey Fischbein-Stepanenko	militiaman
Nina	his niece
Misha-non-penguin	an associate of the Chief
Sonya	his daughter
Sergey Chekalin	"friend" of Misha-non-penguin
Stepan Yakovlevich Pidpaly	a penguinologist
Lyosha	a guard
Ilya Semyonovich	a vet
Valentin Ivanovich	Chairman, Antarctic Committee
Fat Man	

1

First, a stone landed a metre from Viktor's foot. He glanced back. Two louts stood grinning, one of whom stooped, picked up another from a section of broken cobble, and bowled it at him skittler-fashion. Viktor made off at something approaching a racing walk and rounded the corner, telling himself the main thing was not to run. He paused outside his block, glancing up at the hanging clock: 9.00. Not a sound. No one about. He went in, now no longer afraid. They found life dull, ordinary people, now that entertainment was beyond their means. So they bowled cobbles.

As he turned on the kitchen light, it went off again. They had cut the power, just like that. And in the darkness he became aware of the unhurried footfalls of Misha the penguin.

Misha had appeared *chez* Viktor a year before, when the zoo was giving hungry animals away to anyone able to feed them. Viktor had gone along and returned with a king penguin. Abandoned by his girlfriend the week before, he had been feeling lonely. But Misha had brought his own kind of loneliness, and the result was now two complementary lonelinesses, creating an impression more of interdependence than of amity.

Unearthing a candle, he lit it and stood it on the table in an empty mayonnaise pot. The poetic insouciance of the tiny light sent him to look, in the semi-darkness, for pen and paper. He sat down at the table with the paper between him and the candle; paper asking to be written on. Had he been a poet, rhyme would have raced across the white. But he wasn't. He was trapped in a rut between journalism and meagre scraps of prose. Short stories were the best he could do. Very short, too short to make a living from, even if he got paid for them.

A shot rang out.

Darting to the window, Viktor pressed his face to the glass. Nothing. He returned to his sheet of paper. Already he had thought up a story around that shot. A single side was all it took; no more, no less. And as his latest short short story drew to its tragic close, the power came back on and the ceiling bulb blazed. Blowing out the candle, he fetched coley from the freezer for Misha's bowl.

2

Next morning, when he had typed his latest short short story and taken leave of Misha, Viktor set off for the offices of a new fat newspaper that generously published anything, from a cooking recipe to a review of post-Soviet theatre. He knew the Editor, having occasionally drunk with him, and been driven home by his driver afterwards.

The Editor received him with a smile and a slap on the shoulder, told his secretary to make coffee, and there and then gave Viktor's offering a professional read.

"No, old friend," he said eventually. "Don't take it amiss, but it's no go. Needs a spot more gore, or a kinky love angle. Get it into your head that *sensation*'s the essence of a newspaper short story."

Viktor left, without waiting for coffee.

A short step away were the offices of *Capital News*, where, lacking editorial access, he looked in on the Arts section.

"Literature's not actually what we publish," the elderly Assistant Editor informed him amiably. "But leave it with me. Anything's possible. It might get in on a Friday. You know – for balance. If there's a glut of bad news, readers look for something neutral. I'll read it."

Ridding himself of Viktor by handing him his card, the little old man returned to his paper-piled desk. At which point it dawned on Viktor that he had not actually been asked in. The whole exchange had been conducted in the doorway.

3

Two days later the phone rang.

"*Capital News*. Sorry to trouble you," said a crisp, clear female voice. "I have the Editor-in-Chief on the line."

The receiver changed hands.

"Viktor Alekseyevich?" a man's voice enquired. "Couldn't pop in today, could you? Or are you busy?"

"No," said Viktor.

"I'll send a car. Blue *Zhiguli*. Just let me have your address."

Viktor did, and with a "Bye, then," the Editor-in-Chief rang off without giving his name.

Selecting a shirt from the wardrobe, Viktor wondered if it

was to do with his story. Hardly . . . What was his story to them? Still, what the hell!

The driver of the blue *Zhiguli* parked at the entrance was deferential. He it was who conducted Viktor to the Editor-in-Chief.

"I'm Igor Lvovich," he said, extending a hand. "Glad to meet you."

He looked more like an aged athlete than a man of the Press. And maybe that's how it was, except that his eyes betrayed a hint of irony born more of intellect and education than lengthy sessions in a gym.

"Have a seat. Spot of cognac?" He accompanied these words with a lordly wave of the hand.

"I'd prefer coffee, if I may," said Viktor, settling into a leather armchair facing the vast executive desk.

"Two coffees," the Editor-in-Chief said, picking up the phone. "Do you know," he resumed amiably, "we'd only recently been talking about you, and yesterday in came our Assistant Arts Editor, Boris Leonardovich, with your little story. 'Get an eyeful of this,' said he. I did, and it's good. And then it came to me *why* we'd been talking about you, and I thought we should meet."

Viktor nodded politely. Igor Lvovich paused and smiled.

"Viktor Alekseyevich," he resumed, "how about working for us?"

"Writing what?" asked Viktor, secretly alarmed at the prospect of a fresh spell of journalistic hard labour.

Igor Lvovich was on the point of explaining when the secretary came in with their coffee and a bowl of sugar on a tray, and he held his breath until she had gone.

"This is highly confidential," he said. "What we're after is a gifted obituarist, master of the succinct. Snappy, pithy, way-out

4

stuff's the idea. You with me?" He looked hopefully at Viktor.

"Sit in an office, you mean, and wait for deaths?" Viktor asked warily, as if fearing to hear as much confirmed.

"No, of course not! Far more interesting and responsible than that! What you'd have to do is create, from scratch, an index of *obelisk jobs* – as we call obituaries – to include deputies and gangsters, down to the cultural scene – that sort of person – while they're still alive. But what I want is the dead written about as they've never been written about before. And your story tells me you're the man."

"What about payment?"

"You'd start at $300. Hours up to you. But keeping me informed, of course, who we've got carded. So we don't get caught on the hop by some car crash out of the blue! Oh, and one other condition: you'll need a pseudonym. In your own interest as much as anything."

"But what?" said Viktor, half to himself.

"Think of one. But if you can't, make it *A Group of Friends* for the time being."

Viktor nodded.

4

Before bed, he drank tea, and gave not over-serious thought to the subject of death. His mood was of the best, a mood more for vodka than tea. Except that there wasn't any vodka.

What an offer! And though still in the dark concerning his new duties, he had a foretaste of something new and unusual. But

5

roaming the dark corridor, banging every so often against the closed kitchen door, was Misha the penguin. Overcome at last with a feeling of guilt, Viktor let him in. Misha paused at the table, using his almost one metre of height to see what was on it. He looked at the cup of tea, then shifting his gaze to Viktor, considered him with the heartfelt sincerity of a worldly-wise Party functionary. Thinking he would like to give Misha a treat, Viktor went and turned on the cold tap in the bathroom. At the sound of running water Misha came plip-plopping and, without waiting for the bath to fill, leaned over and tumbled in.

The next morning, Viktor looked in at *Capital News* for some practical tips from the Editor-in-Chief.

"How," he asked, "do we select our notables?"

"Nothing easier! See who the papers write about and take your pick. Not all our country's notables are known to it, you see. Many prefer it like that . . ."

That evening Viktor bought all the papers, went home and settled down at the kitchen table.

The very first he looked at gave him food for thought, and the VIP names he underlined he then copied into a notebook *for action*. He would not be short of work – there were 60 or so names from the first few papers alone!

Then tea, and fresh thought, this time concerning the *obelisk* proper. Already he thought he saw how it might be *vitalized*, and at the same time, *sentimentalized*, so that even the simple collective farmer, never having known the late whoever-it-was he was reading about, would brush away a tear. By next morning Viktor had earmarked a possible first *obelisk*. It only remained to get the Chief's blessing.

5

At 9.30 next morning, having got the Chief's blessing, drunk coffee, and been solemnly presented with his Press card, Viktor bought a bottle of Finlandia at a kiosk, and set off for the office of sometime author, now State Duma Deputy, Aleksandr Yakornitsky.

Hearing that a correspondent of *Capital News* wished to see him, the State Deputy was delighted, and immediately told his secretary to cancel all his remaining appointments and admit no one else.

Comfortably ensconced, Viktor put on the table the bottle of Finnish vodka and a dictaphone. Equally promptly, the State Deputy produced two small crystal glasses, placing one either side of the bottle.

He talked freely, without waiting for questions – of his work, his childhood, his time as Komsomol organizer of his university year. As they finished the bottle, he was boasting of his trips to Chernobyl. These, it appeared, had the added bonus of enhancing his potency – as, in case of any doubt, his private-school teacher wife and National Opera diva mistress would testify.

Taking leave of each other, they embraced. Viktor was left with the impression of an author-State-Deputy of great and, for obituary purposes, perhaps undue, vitality. But that was it! Inasmuch as the departed had lately been alive, an obituary should retain their passing warmth – not be all hopeless gloom!

Back at his flat, Viktor wrote the obituary, swiftly *obelisking* the State Deputy in a warm, two-page account of the vital and the sinful, and without recourse to the dictaphone, so fresh was his memory.

"Wonderful job!" Igor Lvovich enthused the next morning.

"Provided singer's hubby keeps his mouth shut . . . *Many women may be mourning him today, but with them in mind, it is to his wife that we shall extend our sympathy; and to one other lady, whose voice, heard by all soaring to the dome of the National Opera, was for him.* Beautiful! Keep it up! On with the good work!"

"Igor Lvovich," began Viktor, growing bolder, "I'm a bit short on facts, and to go interviewing everyone will take time. Have we no carded information?"

The Chief smiled.

"Of course, I was going to suggest it – in *Crime*. I'll tell Fyodor to give you access."

6

As he attuned himself to the task, Viktor's life regulated itself accordingly. He applied himself with a vengeance . . . Fyodor from *Crime* proved a godsend, sharing all that he had, which was plenty – from VIPs' lovers, male and female, to VIPs' lapses from virtue and other life events. In short, from him Viktor gleaned precisely those extra-CV details which, like fine Indian spices, transform an *obelisk* of sad, established fact into a gourmet dish. And each new batch he put regularly before the Chief.

Everything in the garden was lovely. He had money in his pocket – not a lot, but more than enough for his modest requirements. His one occasional anxiety was his lack of recognition, even under a pseudonym, so tenacious of life were his *obelisked* notables. Out of more than 100 written-up VIPs, not only had none of them died, but not one had so much as fallen ill. Such reflections, however, did not affect the rhythm of his work. Assiduously he leafed through the papers, noting names, worming his way into lives. *Our country must know who its notables are*, he kept telling himself.

One rainy November evening, when Misha the penguin was taking a cold bath and Viktor was pondering his subjects' tenacity of life, the phone rang.

"I was put on to you by Igor Lvovich," wheezed a man's voice. "Something I'd like a word about."

At the name of the Editor-in-Chief, Viktor said he would be glad to see him, and half an hour later was welcoming a smartly dressed man of about 45. He had brought a bottle of whisky, and they sat down straight away at the kitchen table.

"I'm Misha," he said, to the amused embarrassment of Viktor.

"Sorry," he explained, "but so's my penguin."

"I've got an old friend who's seriously ill," began the visitor. "Same age as me. Known each other since we were kids. Sergey Chekalin. I'd like to order an obituary . . . Will you do it?"

"Of course," said Viktor. "But I'll need some facts, preferably personal ones."

"No problem," said Misha. "I know all there is to know and can tell you."

"Go ahead."

"Son of a fitter and a nursery governess. His dream, as a child, was to have a motorbike, and when he left school, he bought himself a *Minsk*, though it meant a bit of thieving to do so . . . Deeply ashamed now of his past. Not that his present's any better. We're colleagues, he and I. We set up and we wind up trusts. I'm good at it, he isn't. Wife left him recently. Been alone since. Not even had a lover."

9

"Wife's name?"

"Lena . . . All in all, he's had a rough time of it. Healthwise, too."

"In what way?"

"Suspected stomach cancer, chronic prostate."

"What did he most want out of life?"

"What he'll never have, now: a silver *Lincoln*."

The effect of their cocktail of words and whisky was to render Sergey Chekalin – failure, deserted by wife, ailing, alone and in poor health, dreaming the unrealizable dream of a silver *Lincoln* – a real presence at the table with them.

"When do I come for it?" asked Misha finally.

"Tomorrow, if you like."

He left, and hearing a car start, Viktor looked out and saw a long, pretentious silver *Lincoln* draw away.

He fed Misha freshly frozen plaice, topped up his bath, then returned to the kitchen and set to work on the obituary order. Through the tiny window between bathroom and kitchen he could hear splashing, and as he drafted the *obelisk*, he smiled, thinking of his penguin's love of clean, cold water.

7

Autumn, season of dying nature, of melancholy, of seeking the past, was best for writing obituaries. Winter, joyous in itself – bracing frost, snow sparkling in the sun – was good for living. But till winter came, there were still a few weeks in which to accumulate an *obelisk* surplus for the coming year. There was a lot to do.

When Misha-non-penguin came it was raining again. He read his order, was delighted, and producing his wallet, asked "How much?"

Accustomed so far to monthly payment, Viktor shrugged.

"Look," said Misha, "work well done should be work well paid."

Unable to disagree, Viktor nodded.

Misha thought for a bit.

"Double at least what the priciest whore charges . . . $500 do you?"

Liking the amount, if not the basis of calculation, Viktor nodded, and was handed five $100 bills.

"Can send more clients, if you like," said Misha.

Viktor was all for it.

Misha-non-penguin left. The grey, rainy morning dragged on. The door opened, and there stood Penguin Misha. After a moment he came over and snuggled against his master's knee. Dear creature, thought Viktor, stroking him.

8

Sleeping lightly that night, Viktor heard an insomniac Misha roaming the flat, leaving doors open, occasionally stopping and heaving a deep sigh, like an old man weary of both life and himself.

Next morning Igor Lvovich rang asking him to call in.

Over coffee they discussed the *obelisk* index. On the whole, the Chief was happy.

"One drawback," he said, "is that our future departed all come from Kiev. Being the capital, it does, of course, vacuum up all the more or less notable, but other cities have their quota too."

Viktor listened attentively, now and then nodding.

"We have our own correspondents everywhere, collecting the necessary info," the Chief went on. "It's merely a question of gathering it in. The post's dodgy. Even fax isn't entirely reliable. So what I'd like is for you to come in on it."

"Doing what?"

"Visiting a city or two and collecting. Kharkov, for a start, then, if you wouldn't mind, Odessa. At our expense, naturally . . ."

"I'd be glad to."

Again it was drizzling. On his way home, he dropped into a café, and to get warm, ordered cognac and a large coffee.

The café was empty and quiet – an ambience suitable for dreaming or, conversely, for recalling the past.

He sipped his cognac, his nose prickled by the familiar bouquet, happy in the enjoyment of a drop of the real stuff.

This agreeable café interlude, this stop-off between past and future, over cognac and coffee, induced a mood of romance. No longer did he feel lonely or unhappy. He was a valued customer, satisfying a modest demand for inner warmth. A glass of good cognac and already a flow of warmth in contrary directions: up into his head, down into his legs, and a slowing of thought processes.

He had dreamt once of writing novels, but had not achieved so much as a novella, in spite of all the unfinished manuscripts lying around in folders. But unfinished they were fated to remain, he having been unlucky with his muses, they, for some reason, having never tarried long enough in his two-room flat to see him through a short story. Hence his literary failure. They had been amazingly fickle, his muses. Or he had been at fault for picking such unreliable ones. But now, alone with his penguin, here he was, churning out little pieces regardless, and getting well paid.

Warm at last, he left the café. It was still drizzling. Still a grey, wet day.

Before returning to his flat, he dropped into a shop and bought a kilo of frozen salmon – for Misha.

9

A problem to solve before Kharkov was who to leave Misha with. The odds were that he would happily put up with three days alone, but Viktor was uneasy. Having no friends, he ran through everyone he knew, but they were all people he had little in common with and wasn't keen to approach. Scratching his head, he went over to the window.

It was drizzling. By the entrance, a militiaman was chatting with an old lady from the block. Remembering the joke about the militiaman and the penguin, he smiled, then went over to the phone on the bedside table and looked up the number of the district militiaman.

"Junior Lieutenant Fischbein," came a clipped male voice at the other end of the line.

"Sorry to trouble you," said Viktor hesitantly, searching for words. "There's something I'd like to ask . . . Being resident in your district . . ."

"Trouble?" interrupted the officer.

"No. And don't, please, think I'm trying to be funny. The fact is, I'm going away for three days in connection with work, and I've no one to leave my penguin with."

"Look, I'm sorry," replied the officer in a calm, steady voice, "but living with Mother in a hostel, I've nowhere to keep him . . ."

"You've got me wrong," said Viktor, growing flustered. "What I wondered was whether you could just pop in a couple of times and feed him . . . I'd leave you the keys."

"I could. Name and address, and I'll come round. Will you be in about three?"

"Yes."

He sank into his armchair.

Here, on the broad arm beside him, was where, just over a year ago, petite blonde Olya, of attractive little snub nose and perpetually reproachful expression, was wont to perch. Sometimes she would rest her head on his shoulder and fall asleep, plunging into dreams in which he, very likely, had no place. Only in reality was he allowed to be present. Though even there, he rarely felt needed. Silent and thoughtful – that was her. What, since her pushing off without a word, had altered? Standing beside him now was Misha the penguin. He was silent, but was he thoughtful too? What did being thoughtful amount to? Just a word describing the way one looked, perhaps?

He leant forward, searching the penguin's tiny eyes for signs of thoughtfulness, but saw only sadness.

At 2.45 the district militiaman arrived, taking off his boots inside the door. His appearance belied his surname. He was a broad-shouldered, fair-haired, blue-eyed chap, almost a head taller than Viktor. If he had not been a militiaman, he would have been an asset to any volleyball team.

14

"Well, where is he?" he asked.

"Misha!" Viktor called, and emerging from his hidey-hole behind the dark-green settee, the penguin came and looked the militiaman up and down.

"This, Misha –" began Viktor, and turning to the officer, said, "Sorry, would you tell me your name?"

"Sergey."

"Strange. You don't look at all Jewish."

"Nor am I," smiled the militiaman. "Stepanenko's my real name." With a shrug Viktor turned to the penguin again.

"Misha, this is Sergey. Sergey's going to feed you while I'm away."

He then showed Sergey what was where, and gave him the spare keys to the flat.

"All will be well," said the militiaman as he left. "Don't you worry."

10

Kharkov was freezing, and the moment Viktor stepped from the train, he realized he wasn't dressed warmly enough for strolling round the city.

From his hotel, The Kharkov, he rang the *Capital News* correspondent and they agreed to meet that evening in a café beneath the Opera.

When evening came, he set off on foot along Sumy Street to the Opera, face rimed with frost, hands numb in the pockets of his short sheepskin coat.

The buildings loomed grey over the pavement. Everyone was

in a hurry, as if afraid of finding their block on the verge of collapsing or shedding its balconies – both occurrences being no longer uncommon.

It was another five minutes to the sub-Opera labyrinth of bars, shops and cafés. There he had to locate a café with a stage and seating on two levels, and sit at the front of the upper level, looking towards the stage. And yes, order orange juice and a can of beer, the latter to be left unopened.

Although they had allowed half an hour – from 6.30 till 7.00 – for making contact, he hurried along, spurred on by the cold.

He would get something to eat there, he decided, something hot and meaty . . .

At the Opera he spotted the way down to civilization *sub terra*, away from darkness feebly illuminated by the windows of a nocturnal city, to a blaze of window displays.

On the upper steps two old women and a blurry-faced young drunk stood begging.

Through well-lit corridors he made his way to the café. Inside the glass door sat a man in the uniform of the Special Task Militia, who looked up from his book as Viktor entered.

"And where are *you* going?" he demanded, with only a trace of military insistence.

"To eat."

Special Task Militia waved him on.

He walked the length of a bar at which customers of criminal aspect were drinking beer. The bald-headed barman smiled wryly, catching his eye, as if to say, *Just keep going, don't look back!*

Drawn by bright lights ahead, Viktor quickened his step, and came upon a small stage in a semi-circle of little tables on two levels, one half a metre higher than the other.

He ordered orange juice and a can of beer at the bar.

"That all?" asked the plump, peroxide-blonde barmaid.

"Anything with meat?"

"Cured fish fillet, fried eggs . . ." came the monotone reply.

"All for the moment, then," he said softly.

He paid and took himself to a table on the upper level, facing the stage. One sip of the orange juice made him hungrier than ever. Right, he decided, they would eat at the hotel where there was a restaurant. He consulted his watch: 6.20.

It was quiet. At the next table two Azerbaijanis were drinking beer in silence. Turning to take in the rest of the café, Viktor was momentarily blinded by a flash of light, and when he regained his sight, saw a man with a camera heading for the corridor. He turned to see who had been photographed, but apart from him and the Azerbaijanis, there was no one.

So it was them, he decided, sipping his watery orange.

Time passed. No more than a sip remained in his tall glass. He eyed the unopened can, toying with the idea of getting another, which he would open.

A girl appeared at his table wearing jeans and a leather jacket. Wound tightly about her head was a Rocker scarf, a chestnut ponytail trailing from the knot.

Sitting beside him, she quizzed him through her mascara.

"Waiting for me?" she smiled.

He struggled with embarrassment.

No, the correspondent was a man, was his first fevered thought. Though he might have sent her in his stead . . .

He looked to see if she had a carrier or briefcase such as might have contained the necessary papers, but she had nothing but a vanity bag, too small for even a bottle of beer.

17

"Well, love, how about it? Or haven't you got time?" she asked, reasserting her presence, and the obvious dawned.

"Sorry," said Viktor, "but you're mistaken."

"I'm not often," she said sweetly, rising from the table. "But there's always a first time."

Relieved to be alone again, he took another look at the unopened can, then consulted his watch: 7.15. He should have appeared by now.

But the correspondent did not appear. At 7.30 Viktor drank the beer and left. He ate in the hotel, and returning to his room, again rang the correspondent, but got only long beeps, until he replaced the receiver.

The warmth of the room was relaxing and conducive to sleep. His eyes refused to stay open. He would try again in the morning. That decided, he lay on his bed and slept.

11

In Kiev it was drizzling again. District Militiaman Sergey Fischbein-Stepanenko let himself into Viktor's flat. Removing his boots, he proceeded in knitted green socks to the kitchen, took a large piece of salmon from the freezer, and breaking it across his knee, put half in Misha's bowl on the low, nursery bedside table.

"Misha!" he called, and listened.

Without waiting for a response, he looked into the living room, then into the bedroom, and there found Misha standing, sleepy or sad, between the settee and the wall.

"Grub up!" he cajoled. "Come on!"

Misha stared.

"Come on!" he pleaded. "Master back soon! Of course, you miss him! But come on."

Slowly, followed attentively by Sergey, the penguin dragged himself to the kitchen. Sergey watched him to his bowl, saw him start eating, and returning, conscience clear, to the corridor, put boots and coat back on, and went forth into the Kiev drizzle.

Heaven send a day without call-outs, he thought, seeing the low, louring sky.

12

Woken next morning by a confusion of shots, Viktor yawned, got out of bed and looked at his watch: 8.00. He went over to the window. Parked below, were a militia jeep and an ambulance.

The sky, when he looked up, was blue, and from behind grey Stalin baroque a pale yellow sun had appeared, promising fine weather.

Seated at the telephone table, he dialled the correspondent.

"Who do you want?" a female voice enquired.

"Is Nikolay Aleksandrovich there?"

"Who's calling?"

He sensed tension in the woman's voice. "His paper . . . *Capital News* . . ."

"You are?"

It wasn't right. With a trembling hand he replaced the receiver.

Coffee, must have coffee, he thought, dressing, splashing his face with handfuls of cold water, and going down to the hotel bar where he ordered a large one.

"You sit. I'll bring it," said the barman.

Sitting on a broad soft velour pouffe at a glass-topped table in a corner of the bar, he reached for the heavy glass ashtray, also of cast glass, and twisted it thoughtfully this way and that. The bar was quiet. The barman came with his coffee.

"Anything else?"

He shook his head, then looking squarely at the barman asked, "What was that shooting this morning?"

The barman shrugged.

"Some foreign-currency whore got murdered . . . Must have got up someone's nose."

The coffee, though bitter, proved immediately restorative. His fingers stopped trembling, the throbbing in his head eased. Calm once more, he took stock.

It wasn't the end of the world, he found himself thinking, and with an assurance dismissive of any doubt. That was life. As per usual. Just a question of calling the Chief and asking what to do.

When he had finished his coffee and paid, he went to his room and rang Kiev.

"You've got your return ticket for today," the Chief said calmly. "So back you come. Carry on with Kiev. The provinces can hang fire for a bit."

Taking his seat on the night train, Viktor opened the *Evening Kharkov* he had bought at the station. As he turned the pages, he came to a *Criminal Chronicle* setting forth, in small print, all the most recent crimes, and under *Murders*, read:

> *Capital News* correspondent Nikolay Agnivtsev was shot dead at his flat yesterday afternoon by persons unknown.

With a sick feeling, he lowered the paper to his knees. The train gave a sudden jolt and the paper slid to the floor.

13

On the way up to his flat the next morning, Viktor met the district militiaman.

"Good day to you!" said Sergey Fischbein-Stepanenko gaily. "You're looking a bit pale, though."

"How is he?" asked Viktor anxiously.

"In fine shape!" said the militiaman with a smile. "Missing his master, of course. And your freezer's out of fish."

"I can't thank you enough." His attempt at a grateful smile produced a sickly sour grimace. "I'm in your debt. How about raising a glass together some time?"

"Wouldn't say no," confirmed the militiaman. "Just ring – you've got my number. And if you need me again, don't hesitate! I love animals. Real ones, I mean, not the sort I deal with every day . . ."

Misha, standing in the corridor, was delighted to see Viktor come in and turn on the light.

"Hello, old fellow." Viktor squatted and looked at him.

He seemed to be smiling.

And as he took a lumbering step towards his master, he had a happy twinkle in his eye.

At least someone in this world's glad to see me, thought Viktor.

Straightening up, he removed his jacket and went through to the living room, Misha plip-plopping behind him.

14

Next morning Viktor lay in bed with a headache and no inclination to get up.

The alarm clock showed 9.30.

Heaving himself over onto his other side, he became aware of Misha standing by his bed.

"Oh God!" he muttered, swinging his feet to the floor, "I've not fed him since yesterday!"

And in spite of his splitting head and buzzing temples, he washed and dressed.

The frosty air perked him up a little. Winter seemed to have followed him from Kharkov.

Must phone the Chief, he decided as he walked, say I'm unwell . . . Get the papers, and maybe do a bit of work . . .

At the fish counter of the food store he purchased two kilos of frozen plaice; then, after a moment's hesitation, a kilo of live fish.

Back at his flat he ran a bath of cold water, released the three silver carp, and called Misha. Misha took one look at the fish swimming in the bath, turned away, and plip-plopped back to his room. Viktor shrugged. He was at a loss.

The doorbell rang.

Espying Misha-non-penguin through the peephole, he let him in.

"Hi," said Misha. "Got a couple of obituary orders for you. You all right?"

Viktor gestured vaguely.

They went through to the kitchen, just as the penguin came plip-plopping that way.

"Hi, namesake!" grinned the visitor, then, looking at Viktor, asked, "Why so gloomy? You off colour or something?"

"Yes. Everything's bloody . . ."

He felt like having a moan, although something inside him protested that he shouldn't.

"Here I am, writing and writing, but nobody sees what I write," he declared, more in anger than in a bid for sympathy. "Two hundred pages to date. And all for nothing."

"What do you mean *for nothing*?" interrupted Misha-non-penguin. "You – like so many in the good old Soviet days – are writing *for the drawer*. With the difference that you, sooner or later, *are* going to be published . . . *That* I guarantee."

Unsmiling and unrelenting, Viktor acknowledged as much with a nod.

"Who do you reckon you've done best by?" Misha-non-penguin asked amiably.

"Yakornitsky," said Viktor, recalling their lengthy, Finnish-vodka-assisted table talk.

"The author-State-Deputy?"

"That's him."

"Right," said Misha. "And here's something of interest for you. Have a look at that lot."

Viktor glanced at the several pages: names he was unfamiliar with, biographical details, dates. Not what he felt like immersing himself in just then. With a nod of thanks he laid them aside.

"Ring when you're ready," Misha-non-penguin said, handing him his card.

15

The first snow was falling. Viktor was reading, over coffee, what Misha-non-penguin had brought a couple of days before: files on the Deputy Head of the Taxation Service and the Manageress of The Carpathians. The lives of this pair were garish enough to make quite exceptional obelisks. With characters like them – anti-heroes of the first water – a thriller would write itself! Except that novel-writing called for unlimited free time, which Viktor didn't have. True, what he did have now was money, Penguin Misha, and three silver carp in the bathroom. But was he to regard all that as compensation for an unwritten novel?

Reminded of the carp, he fetched a piece of bread and went to the bathroom to feed them.

He had just crumbled the bread, when he heard breathing beside him. He turned and saw Misha gazing dolefully at the fish in the bath.

"Don't care for freshwater fish, is that it?" he asked. "But of course!" he continued, supplying his own answer. "We creatures of Antarctic and of ocean . . ."

Going to the phone, he rang the militiaman and invited him to a fish supper.

It was still snowing.

He put his typewriter on the kitchen table, and word by word, set about painting vital images of the future departed.

Slowly but surely the work advanced, every word as rock solid as the base of an Egyptian pyramid.

> Much against his will, the departed acquiesced in the mur-
> der of his younger brother, the latter having chanced upon

a list of shareholders of an as yet unprivatized washing-machine factory. However, the monument erected by the deceased in memory of his brother has become a veritable adornment of the cemetery. Often life makes it necessary to kill, while the death of someone close makes it necessary to live on regardless . . . Everything in this world is united by virtue of blood. The life of all is a single whole, and for that reason the death of one small part of the whole still leaves life behind it, since the number of living parts always exceeds the number of deceased . . .

District Militiaman Fischbein-Stepanenko came to supper wearing jeans and a black sweater over a striped flannel shirt, carrying a bottle of cognac and a bag of frozen fish for the penguin.

Supper being still in the making, they together set about frying the former occupants of the bath. Misha, meanwhile, was in the bathroom, splashing about in fresh cold water. Viktor and Sergey could hear him above the sizzling of the fish in the frying pan, and exchanged smiles.

At last the meal was ready.

Host and guest downed a cognac before addressing themselves to the fish.

"Bony," said Viktor, as if apologizing on the fishes' behalf.

"Not to worry," said the militiaman shaking his head. "Everything has its price . . . The bonier the fish, the better the flavour. I remember I once tried whale. That's fish too, of course! No bones, but no flavour either . . ."

They helped the fish down with cognac, watching whirling snowflakes lit by the dim light of other people's windows.

25

Their supper had a touch of New Year about it.

"Why do you live alone?" asked Sergey, in the new intimacy of having drunk to their friendship.

Viktor shrugged. "It's the way it's been. No luck with women. They've always been the otherworldly sort. Quiet. Mousy. Here today, gone tomorrow . . . Got me down. I took on Misha, and somehow things improved. Except that he's always down in the dumps for some reason . . . Better perhaps to have got a dog . . . They're more emotional: bark when they see you, lick you, wag their tails . . ."

"Think so?" Sergey waved dismissively. "Two walks a day . . . Stinking the flat out . . . Better off with a penguin. But you, what do you do?"

"I write."

"For children?"

"Why *for children*?" asked Viktor in surprise. "No, for a newspaper."

"Ah," Sergey shook his head. "Don't care for newspapers. They always upset you."

"I don't care for them either. – But where, if you don't mind my asking, did the *Fischbein* come from?"

Sergey gave a deep sigh.

"From being bored and having an aunt in *Documents*. I thought one day I'd turn Jew, and get the hell out of it. So I just wrote, like Auntie said, *reporting loss of identity card*, and she made me out a new one in a new name. Seeing later how unenviably émigrés from here lived abroad, I thought I'd stay, and to get myself a weapon, went into the militia. It's a safe job, basically: sorting out domestic brawls and every sort of bloody fool complaint. Not quite what I dreamt of, of course."

"And what was that?"

At this point the door opened, and Misha the penguin appeared, dripping water. He stood for a moment, then, marching past the table to his bowl, looked quizzically at his master. The bowl was empty.

Viktor went to the freezer, and breaking three plaice from the frozen mass, cut them up and put them in the bowl.

Misha rested his head against the frozen fish.

"He's thawing it!" cried Sergey, watching with interest. "He really is!"

Returning to his chair, Viktor watched, too.

"Well, that's it," said Sergey, reaching for his glass. "We all of us deserve better fish, but eat what we've got . . . So, here's to friendship!"

Clinking glasses, they drank. And Viktor felt a sudden sense of relief. Past dissatisfaction with himself and others was wholly forgotten, and with it, his *obelisks*. It was as though he had never worked anywhere, but just lived, planning a novel which some day he would write. Looking at Sergey, he was moved to smile. Friendship. Something he had never had. Any more than a three-piece suit, or real passion. Life had been pale, sickly and joyless. Even Misha was down in the dumps, as if he, too, knew only a pallid life devoid of colours, emotions, delight, and joyous splashings of the soul.

"Look, let's have another," Sergey suggested suddenly, "then go for a walk, all three of us."

It was late and quiet. All children were long since in bed, the street lamps were off, only the odd light and the occasional lighted window lit the newly fallen first snow.

They slowly made their way to the waste area where there

27

were three dovecotes, cheeks stung by the frosty air, snow crunching underfoot.

"Behold!" cried Sergey, striding towards a figure in a shabby overcoat recumbent in the snow beneath one of the dovecotes. "Your neighbour Polikarpov from Flat 30, who, if he's not to freeze to death, must be lugged into the nearest block and parked against a radiator."

Grasping him by his coat collar, they dragged the drunken Polikarpov through the snow to the nearest five-storey block, Misha waddling behind.

When they came out, they found Misha and a massive mongrel standing nose to nose, each, apparently, sniffing the other. Seeing them, the dog ran off.

16

The next morning Viktor was woken by the phone.

"Hello?" he answered in a husky, half-awake voice.

"Congratulations, Viktor Alekseyevich! You're off the mark! Didn't wake you, did I?"

"Time I was up anyway," said Viktor, recognizing the Chief's voice. "What's the trouble?"

"You're in print! And how are you feeling, by the way?"

"Better already."

"Call in, then. We'll talk."

Viktor washed, breakfasted, drank tea, looked in on Misha and found him standing asleep in his favourite hidey-hole behind the dark-green settee.

Returning to the kitchen he put a large piece of frozen cod in Misha's bowl, dressed and went out.

Outside lay a fresh fall of snow. A blue-grey sky was pressing down almost to the rooftops of the five-storey blocks. There was no wind and it was not very cold.

Before boarding the bus, he had bought the latest *Capital News*, and having secured a comfortable seat, he opened it out and scanned the headlines, coming at last to a rectangle of text set high on the page and framed heavily in black.

> Writer and State Deputy Aleksandr Yakornitsky is no longer with us. In the third row of the Chamber, a leather seat stands empty. To be occupied, before long, by another. But in the hearts of the many who knew Aleksandr Yakornitsky there will be a sense of emptiness, of profound loss . . .

So there it was, his first publication.

But he did not feel particularly happy, despite the long-forgotten sense of personal satisfaction that stirred deep down. He read through to the end. Every word in place, no sign of a cut.

His eye rested on the signature – *A Group of Friends* – more like a phrase than a pseudonym, the four words serving as an umbrella for any number. The funny thing was that this was exactly how he had typed it, both nouns with a capital. And even this the Editor had left, treating Viktor more like a respected writer than a journalist.

Lowering the paper, he looked out at the approaching city.

"Look, a little bird!" said a mother sitting in front of him with her child, and pointing. Glancing automatically in the direction indicated, he saw a sparrow fluttering inside the bus.

17

The Editor-in-Chief greeted Viktor cordially, as if he had not seen him for a year. Coffee, cognac and $100 in a long elegant envelope made their appearance. It was quite a celebration.

"Well," said Igor Lvovich, raising his glass of cognac, "a start's been made. Let's hope our remaining *obelisks* don't hang around for long either."

"How did he die?" Viktor asked.

"Fell from a sixth-floor window – was cleaning it for some reason, apparently, though it wasn't his. And at night."

Clinking glasses, they drank.

"Do you know," the Chief confided further, "I've had colleagues from other papers ringing. Green with envy, the parasites! I, they say, have invented a new kind of obituary!" He smiled smugly. "The credit's all yours, of course. But you being *under wraps*, I take the compliments, and the kicks! OK?"

Viktor nodded, though he was secretly pained at being kept out of the limelight, fame still being fame, albeit journalistic. Something of which became apparent to the Chief from Viktor's expression.

"Don't take it to heart. Everyone will know your real name some day – if you want . . . But for the moment, best keep to the *Group of Friends* that no one knows. You'll see why in a day or two. And incidentally, don't forget: everything underlined in the files from Fyodor, *you're to use*. I don't cut your philosophizings, do I? Even though they have, quite frankly, damn all to do with the late lamented."

Viktor nodded his agreement. He sipped his coffee, and was

reminded suddenly, by the bitterish flavour, of the hotel bar in Kharkov and the morning he had been woken by shooting.

"What did happen in Kharkov, Igor?" he asked.

Sighing, the Chief poured cognac and gave Viktor an inhibited, arrested sort of look.

"Bowed his head did our brave young Red,"

he crooned softly:

"Cruelly shot through his Komsomol heart . . .

"As a newspaper, we've had our losses. This one's our seventh. Before long we'll be unveiling a pantheon . . . Still, no skin off your nose! The less you know, the longer you live!" said the Chief. Then, in quite a different, somehow weary voice, and looking hard at him, he added "And it's not your business any longer. Just that you know a bit more than others do . . . OK . . ."

Viktor regretted his curiosity. The whole ambience of their little tête à tête celebration had been lost.

18

The end of November saw the transition from deep autumn to deep winter. Children threw snowballs. An icy chill crept under coat collars. Cars drove slowly, as if frightened of each other, the roads being now much narrower. The cold diminished, shortened, shrivelled everything. The kerbside mounds of snow were the only things to grow, and these only by virtue of the hard work and broad shovels of the clearers of courtyards and pavements.

Having completed the second of Misha-non-penguin's *obelisks*,

Viktor looked out of the window. Today had been a day when he had neither wanted nor needed to go out. To break the silence, he switched on the set-programme speaker standing on the fridge. The carefree hubbub of parliament (plus hiss) burst forth. He turned down the volume, put the kettle on for tea, and glanced at his watch: 5.30. A bit early to be finishing for the day.

He rang Misha-non-penguin.

"All ready," he reported. "Come and collect."

Misha came, but not alone. With him was a little girl with round inquisitive eyes.

"My daughter," he said. "No one to leave her with . . . Tell Uncle Vik your name." He stooped to unbutton her little coat of reddish fur.

"Sonya," she said gazing up at him. "And I'm four. – Have you really got a penguin living here?"

"You see? And she's hardly been here a minute . . ." He removed her coat and helped her off with her little boots.

They went through to the living room.

"Where is he?" she asked, looking round.

"I'll go and see," said Viktor, but first he fetched Misha-non-penguin the two new *obelisks* from the kitchen.

"Misha," he called, looking behind the dark-green settee.

Misha, standing in his hidey-hole on a treble thickness of camel-hair blanket, was staring at the wall.

"All right?" Viktor asked, stooping down to him.

The penguin stood staring wide-eyed.

Viktor wondered if he was ill.

"What's wrong with him?" asked Sonya, having crept to join them.

"Misha! We've got visitors!"

Sonya went over and stroked the penguin.

"Are you feeling bad?" she asked.

Misha jerked round and looked at her.

"Daddy!" she cried, "He moved!"

Leaving them together, Viktor retired to the living room. Misha-non-penguin, deep in an armchair, was getting to the end of the second obituary. From the look on his face he seemed pleased.

"Good stuff!" he said. "Touching. Absolute shits, that's clear, but reading this, one feels sorry for them . . . Any tea going?"

They moved to the kitchen, and while waiting for the kettle, sat at the table talking of the weather and other trivial matters. Tea made and poured, Misha-non-penguin handed Viktor an envelope.

"Your honorarium," he said. "And there's another client coming. – Oh, and you remember the one you did for Sergey Chekalin?"

Viktor nodded.

"He's recovered . . . I faxed him your effort. I think he liked it . . . Anyway, he was impressed!"

"Daddy, Daddy," came the little girl's voice, "he's hungry!"

"So he can talk, can he?" grinned Misha-non-penguin.

Viktor took cod from the freezer and put it in the bowl.

"Sonya, tell him food's on the table," he called.

"Hear that?" They could faintly heard her telling him. "You're to come to table."

The penguin arrived first, trailed by Sonya. Following him to his bowl, she watched with interest as he ate.

"Why's he on his own?" she asked suddenly, looking up.

"Oh, I don't know," said Viktor. "Actually he isn't. We live here together."

33

"Like me and Daddy," said Sonya.

"What a chatterbox!" sighed Misha-non-penguin, gulping tea and contemplating his daughter. "Come on, time to go home."

Thoroughly dejected, she left the kitchen.

"Have to get her a puppy or a cat," said Misha-non-penguin, watching her go.

"Bring her again, to play," Viktor suggested.

Outside, the inky blackness of a winter evening. Barely audibly, the set-programme speaker was reporting events in Chechnya. Viktor sat at the typewriter at the kitchen table, feeling lonely. He would have liked to write a short story – or a fairy story – even if just for Sonya. But filling his head was the mournful, heartfelt melody of an as yet unwritten *obelisk*.

"Am I ill?" he wondered, staring at the blank paper protruding from the typewriter. "No, I must, must, sometimes at least, make myself write short stories, or else I'll go mad."

He fell to thinking of Sonya's funny little freckled face, her red ponytail with its elastic band.

Odd times to be a child in. An odd country, an odd life which he had no desire to make sense of. To endure, full stop, that was all he wanted.

19

A few days later the Chief rang, telling him to be more on his guard, and not to come to the office or go out for the time being, unless he had to.

Puzzled, Viktor kept the receiver to his ear for a minute's

worth of short beeps. What had happened, he wondered, still hearing the calm, self-assured, professorial voice of the Chief. He shrugged. He couldn't take it seriously, that call. But his morning acquired, unaided, two profitless hours. He spent a long time shaving, and ironing, for no good reason, a shirt he had no intention of wearing.

Towards midday he sallied forth, bought papers, popped into the food store for fish for Misha and for himself, together with a kilo of bananas.

Back at the flat he scanned the papers, but they provided no answer to the Chief's call. However, new names caught his eye, and fetching his notebook, he duly entered them, to work on in the future, only not now. He was in a state of complete enervation. Sitting at the kitchen table on which reposed his bag of shopping, he extracted a banana.

The kitchen door creaked open. Misha the penguin came in and stood in front of his master, looking pleadingly at him.

Viktor held out the banana he was eating.

Misha leant forward and bit a piece off.

"Think you're a monkey, do you?" exclaimed Viktor. "But you watch it! If you go poisoning yourself, where do we find a doctor? We haven't enough to cope with us humans! I'd better give you some fish."

The silence of the kitchen was broken by the sound of Misha tackling his cod, and the breathing of a profoundly pensive Viktor. At last, with a sigh, he got up and turned on the speaker. Militia siren. It must be a radio play. But no. It was a report *from the scene of battle*, this time at the intersection of Red Army and Saksagansky Streets, practically in the city centre. He turned up the volume. An agitated account of pools of blood on the road, three ambulances taking 30 minutes to arrive, seven bodies, five wounded. First indications were that among the dead was the Deputy Sports Minister, State Deputy Stoyanov. Turning automatically to his notebook, Viktor checked: the newly departed Stoyanov was there. With a nod of satisfaction he resumed listening, leaving his notebook open. But the reporter proceeded to repeat the facts already given, these, apparently, being all he knew. He would, he promised, be back in half an hour with further details, and a pleasantly spoken woman took over with a weather forecast for the weekend.

Saturday tomorrow, thought Viktor, and turned to look at Misha.

Working from home, he had lost any sense of distinction between working and non-working days: working if he felt like it, or not, if he didn't. Mostly though, he did feel like it. It was just that he had nothing further to work on. As to writing stories, starting a novella or even a novel, that had not come off. It was as if he had found his *genre* and was so constrained by its limits that even when not writing *obelisks*, he was thinking *obelisks*, or thoughts so elegant and attuned to mourning that they could be slotted, by way of a philosophical digression, into any obituary – and sometimes were.

He rang the District Militiaman.

"Lieutenant Fischbein," came the clear, familiar voice.

"Hi, Sergey. Vik."

"Vik?"

"Master of Misha."

"Why didn't you say? What's new? How is he?" was the cheery response.

"He's OK. Look, are you off-duty tomorrow?"

"Yes."

36

"Got a bright idea, and wonder if you're game," said Viktor hopefully. "All we need is a vehicle. A militia jeep would do . . ."

"If it's not in furtherance of a punishable offence, no problem . . ." laughed Sergey. "But why a jeep, when I've got my own *Zaporozhets*?"

20

In the icy cold of Saturday morning, Viktor, Sergey and Penguin Misha emerged from a red *Zaporozhets* parked on the Dnieper Embankment near the Monastery Gardens. Sergey collected a bulging rucksack from the boot, shouldered it, and they descended the stone steps to the frozen river.

The Dnieper was under a thick layer of ice, on which, at polite distances from one another, the winter anglers sat like fat, motionless crows, each by his own hole.

Steering clear of them, Viktor, Sergey and Misha headed deep into the Dnieper ice fields.

They paused at every free hole, but they were all either frozen over or too small.

"Let's try the bay," said Sergey. "Where winter swimmers go."

They made towards a narrow spit, the tail of an island, which they crossed.

"There, look!" said Sergey pointing. "See that patch of blue?"

The hole, when they reached it, was vast, with many naked heel-prints at its edge. Without waiting for the go-ahead, Misha lunged forward and dived smoothly in without so much as a splash.

Viktor and Sergey stared at the heaving mash of ice and water, hardly daring to breathe.

"Can they see under water?" Sergey asked.

"I daresay," said Viktor. "If there's anything to see."

Taking off his rucksack, Sergey pulled out an old quilt, which he spread on the ice a metre or two from the hole.

"Come and sit down," he called. "Each to his own holiday amusement."

Viktor came and sat, Sergey having meanwhile produced a thermos and two plastic cups.

"We'll start with coffee."

It was sweet, and made a pleasant drink against the cold.

"And I never thought to bring anything," Viktor confessed sadly, warming his hands around his cup.

"Never mind, there'll be another time. Spot of cognac?"

Sergey poured some into each cup, then slipped the flat bottle into a jacket pocket.

"To all that's good!" he proposed.

They drank, warmth pervading their bodies and minds.

"He won't drown, will he?" Sergey asked, looking towards the ice-hole.

"He shouldn't," shrugged Viktor. "But I'm in the dark really about penguins. I've looked for books on them, but haven't found any."

"If I come across anything, you shall have it," Sergey promised.

Viktor looked around anxiously. The nearest angler and hole were a good 30 metres away. The angler was sitting on his tackle box and every now and then could be seen raising a litre-sized water bottle to his lips.

"Think I'll take a stroll," said Viktor, still watching the angler.

"I shouldn't. Let's sit for a bit and have some more cognac. He'll be back. He won't drown, that's for sure!"

A sudden gurgling came from the ice-hole. Viktor looked at once, but it was only the mash of ice and water slopping to and fro.

Sergey raised his cup of cognac. "Come, let's drink to him. People are legion, penguins are not – and ought to be cherished!"

As they drank, a cry rent the frosty silence. Swinging round, they saw an angler some 50 metres away leap back from his hole, pointing at it with both hands. Two other anglers were heading his way, abandoning their rods in their holes.

"What's up with him?" Sergey asked, speaking to himself.

Oblivious to events 50 metres away, Viktor was sipping his cognac and considering how each new day brought to one's life something new, totally unplanned for. A time would come when it would be trouble of some sort, perhaps even death.

"Look!" shouted Sergey, clapping him on the shoulder.

Returning to the here and now, Viktor looked first at Sergey, then, following his gaze, saw Misha approaching from the direction of the island.

"Where's he popped up from?" asked Sergey in amazement.

Misha came to a halt at the edge of their quilt.

"Perhaps he'd like a cognac," quipped Sergey.

"Come on, Misha," called Viktor, patting the quilt.

Misha stepped awkwardly onto it and looked from one to the other of them.

Reaching once more into his rucksack, Sergey produced a towel and wrapped it around him.

"So he doesn't catch cold," he explained.

Misha stood in his towel for five minutes or so, then threw it off.

Hearing footsteps, Viktor turned.

It was the owner of the nearest hole.

"Fish biting?" asked Sergey.

Eyes fixed on the penguin, the fisherman shook his head.

"Look," he said at last, "is that a penguin you've got there, or am I seeing things?"

"You're seeing things," Sergey assured him firmly.

"Christ!" he whispered, aghast.

With an ungainly wave of his arms, he turned and set off back to his hole.

"Now, perhaps he'll ease off the drink a bit," said Sergey hopefully, as they watched him go.

"You're not on duty now," Viktor reproached him. "Why go scaring drunks to death?"

"Professional instinct," said Sergey with a smile. "Like something to eat? Or shall we have another first?"

"We'll have another first."

Suddenly Misha began marking time impatiently, flapping his flippers.

"Think he needs a bog?" Sergey grinned, unscrewing the cognac.

Misha, having meanwhile abandoned quilt for ice, set off at a comical waddling run and dived once more into the ice-hole.

21

In the small hours of Monday morning, Viktor was roused by the insistent ringing of the phone. When finally awake, he didn't feel like getting up, but lay waiting for the caller to lose patience.

But the caller didn't lose patience, and even the penguin woke and gabbled.

Viktor got out of bed and made his way unsteadily to the phone.

Some idiot's idea of a joke! he thought, lifting the receiver.

"Vik?" It was the Chief and he sounded impatient. "Sorry to wake you. Urgent job! Are you listening?"

"Yes."

"A courier's on his way with an envelope. He'll wait in his car while you get cracking on the *obelisk*. It's for the morning edition."

Viktor glanced at the alarm clock on the bedside table. It was 1.30.

"All right."

He put on his blue towelling dressing-gown, washed in cold water, then proceeded to the kitchen. Here he put the kettle on the stove, his typewriter on the table, and listened to the silence of the night. He looked out at the block opposite. Only two lighted windows in the whole building.

Not his problem, other people's insomnia. He was his waking self again, except for a heavy head. He fetched paper, inserted it in the typewriter, and again listened to the silence of the night.

A car drew up outside. A door banged.

He waited patiently for the doorbell. A short while later, instead of a ring, there was a guarded knock.

A red-eyed, sleepy-looking man of about 50 handed him a large brown envelope.

"I'm down in the car. Hammer on the door if I'm asleep," he said, without coming in.

Sitting at his typewriter, Viktor drew from the envelope a sheet of paper and a theatre programme.

> Parkhomenko, Yuliya Andreyevna, b. 1955. Since 1988,
> singer Nat. Opera. Married, two children.

he read.

> 1991, mastectomy. 1993, summoned as witness re
> disappearance of Nat. Opera diva Sanuchenko, Irina
> Fyodorovna, who she was at daggers drawn with. 1995
> opted out of planned Italian tour, nearly aborting it.

Followed by the handwritten addendum:

> Severely affected by death of Nikolay Aleksandrovich
> Yakornitsky, author, State Deputy, and (since 1994 and
> her appearance at a private celebration of Ukrainian
> Independence at the Mariynsky Palace) her most intimate
> friend.

This underlined in red pencil, at once recalled his last conversation with Igor Lvovich.

He read it a number of times. Not much to go on, but already
his thoughts were attuned to the requisite degree of pathos.

On page two of the programme he discovered a colour
photograph of the singer: a comely, shapely lady, with flushed,
undoubtedly rouged cheeks; almond eyes; chestnut hair cascading
over shoulders; revealing costume.

Back to blank sheet in typewriter.

For Arabs, white was the colour of mourning, he reflected,
fingers poised above the keys.

> All that is possessed of life in this world has a voice of its
> own. The voice is a sign of life. It may grow in strength,
> break off, be lost, sink to a barely audible whisper. In the

chorus of our lives the individual voice is not easily distinguished, but where, suddenly, it falls silent, there comes an awareness of the finitude of any sound, of any life. One voice that we are given to hear no more is a voice that has been loved by many . . . Suddenly, prematurely, it has been lost. To which extent the world has become more silent, though not as sought by lovers of tranquillity. The silence now fallen serves, like a black hole in the universe, only to emphasize the finitude of any sound and the infinity of past and future losses . . .

Getting up, Viktor went and made tea, returning with a large cup.

. . . The voice of Yuliya Parkhomenko is now silent. But so long as the walls of the Mariynsky Palace endure, and the splendour of the National Opera is reflected in the gold of its inner cupola, she will abide as a golden haze dissolved upon the air we breathe. Her voice will be the gilding of the silence she has left behind.

A bit too much gold, he thought, pausing. Again he picked up the sheet of notes, and for the umpteenth time perused the underlinings. How was he to bring in Yakornitsky? Love? Love . . .

Gulping tea, he pondered the point. He read what he had written, before continuing:

She suffered, not long ago, the grievous loss of the voice of one dear to her. Silenced abruptly it was, that voice, lost as a dying fall into that abyss, whither, by Death's Laws of Gravity descends all that, having fought the good fight, or simply lost out, has had its day.

Here, breaking off again to look more closely at the programme, he permitted himself the ghost of a smile.

> Only recently, as *Tosca* in Puccini's opera, she acted out
> her own tragedy to the full in her final leap from the
> battlements. The manner of her death is not of impor-
> tance. Had it been of a different order, we who have given
> ear to her life would still face the difficult task of now
> accustoming ourselves to silence, and seeking therein
> golden traces of her late presence. Let us, therefore, all
> fall silent, the better to distinguish her voice – distinguish,
> recall and cherish in memory until our own voices are
> mingled with silence and eternity . . .

He straightened up, breathing hard, as if having completed
a 100-metre sprint, not sat tapping away at a typewriter. To relieve
the strain imposed by this urgent nocturnal commission, he
massaged his temples. Still, the job was done.

He reached for what he had written and read it through, feeling
suddenly sorry for the opera singer who had died, or met death,
he knew not how.

He looked out of the window. The car was down below, waiting.

Getting to his feet, he turned, and was startled to see Misha
looking on thoughtfully from the doorway, standing immobile,
tiny eyes alone burning with vital fire, but quite inscrutable,
simply observing his master dispassionately, and for no particular
reason.

Taking a deep breath, Viktor squeezed between penguin
and door and out into the corridor, threw his sheepskin jacket
over his dressing-gown, and made for the landing and stairs,
clutching his text.

The courier was asleep, head sunk forward onto the wheel. Viktor tapped the window. The man rubbed his eyes. Without a word, he opened the door, relieved Viktor of the page of text, started the engine and drove off.

Viktor returned to his flat. The night was all in pieces. He didn't feel like sleep, he was brimming with superfluous energy.

Discovering some sleeping tablets in the medicine cabinet, he washed down two with water still warm from the kettle, and retired to his room.

22

Next morning at ten, the Chief rang again. He was happy with the *obelisk* and apologized once more for disturbing Viktor's sleep. A couple more days, he said, and Viktor would be able to come to the office, the main thing being to remember his Press card, as the Special Task Militia was now on duty at the entrance and on every floor.

Outside, winter continued crisp with frost. It was fairly quiet.

Standing over his Turkish coffee-maker at the stove, Viktor was wondering how to fill his day. One possibility, in view of his night's work, was take the day off. But a day off involved an even greater need for interesting content than a normal day. He therefore decided to go, after coffee, to the kiosk for the papers, and then make up his mind what to do.

His second cup he drank over the papers. First, he read his night's work, now in half a million copies, on the last page but one. It was all there, untouched by the Editor-in-Chief. *He* would have been enjoying his night's sleep while the text was being set ready for the press. Going back to page one, he read the lengthy, full-page leader: NOT AN END TO WAR BUT A TRUCE. Pictures reminiscent of the assault on Grozny broke up the soldierly columns of print. He ploughed on. The more he read, the more absorbed he became. What emerged was that while he had been leading a normal life in Kiev, near-battles had been fought by two warring Mafia clans. At least, so the article claimed. Seventeen dead, nine wounded, five bomb blasts. Among the dead were the Editor-in-Chief's driver, three militiamen, an Arab businessman, persons as yet unidentified, and a singer from the National Opera.

The other papers, he noticed, devoted far less space to the *war* than *Capital News*. Against that, there was a little more about the death of the singer, whose body had been discovered in the early hours at the lower funicular station. She had been strangled with a leather belt. Furthermore, her architect husband had vanished and their flat was in disorder, having evidently been ransacked in search of something.

Viktor pondered. The singer's death had, on the face of it, nothing to do with clan warfare. A completely *extraneous* crime, in fact. The missing husband might have had a hand in it. And – the thought horrified him – so might *he*, having referred to her in his Yakornitsky obituary. He had not named her, of course, but for many a nod was as good as a wink, and that might have been the last straw for hubby . . .

He sighed, and for a moment felt appallingly wearied by his own assumptions.

"What rubbish!" he said under his breath. "Why would hubby ransack his own flat?"

23

The day ended, oddly enough, on a fairly productive note. Three *obelisks* lay ready on the table. Through the window the light of the winter evening was fading. Steam was rising from a freshly made cup of tea.

He skimmed his latest efforts. A bit on the short side, but all because he had not been to the office for some time for additional information on his notables from Fyodor. But that was no problem. Pending printing he could still work on them, still revise them.

He drank his tea, turned off the kitchen light, and was on his way to bed, when there was a knock at the door.

Taken aback, Viktor stood in the corridor listening to the silence. Then, discarding his slippers, he went barefoot to the door and peeped through the spyhole. It was Misha-non-penguin. Viktor let him in.

Misha had Sonya in his arms, asleep. He came in without a word, merely nodding hello.

"Where can I put her?"

"In there," whispered Viktor indicating the living room door.

Misha laid Sonya on the settee, then tiptoed back to the corridor.

"Let's go to the kitchen," he suggested.

On again went the kitchen light.

"Put the kettle on."

"It's only just boiled."

"I'll stay till morning," Misha said dully. "And Sonya can live here for a bit . . . OK? Till things settle down."

"What things?" asked Viktor.

47

But he received no answer. They were sitting opposite each other at the kitchen table, except that Misha was now where Viktor usually sat, and Viktor had his back to the stove. For just an instant he seemed to detect a flash of hostility in Misha's eyes.

"Cognac?" he asked, in an effort to lift the black cloud of tension hanging over them.

"All right," said his visitor.

Viktor poured. They drank in silence.

Lost in thought, Misha drummed the table with his fingers. Looking around and spotting the pile of newspapers on the window sill, he drew it towards him. Picking up the topmost, he pulled a wry face and thrust the papers back again.

"Life's funny," he sighed. "You try to give pleasure and end up crash-diving like a submarine . . ."

Viktor heard what he was saying, but the meaning eluded him, like gossamer in the wind.

"Pour me another," said Misha.

Downing his second glass, he went and looked at Sonya still peacefully asleep in the living room, then came back.

"I daresay you'd like to know what's happened," he said slowly in a weaker voice, looking hard at Viktor.

Viktor said nothing. He no longer wanted to know anything. Sleep was what he wanted, and Misha-non-penguin's odd behaviour was beginning to get him down.

"The shootings, the bombs, you know about, don't you." Misha gestured towards the papers.

"Well?" asked Viktor.

"Know who's to blame for that lot?"

"Who?"

Misha combined a longish pause with a smile that was weary and unfriendly.

"You."

"*Me?* How – how could I?"

"Not entirely you, of course . . . Though without you, none of this would have happened." He stared unblinkingly, seeming to gaze through and beyond Viktor. "Just that you were feeling bloody – I could see you were. I asked you why. You told me. We were open about it. That child-like openness was what I liked about you. You wanted to see your little bits in print, edged round with black. And why not? So then I asked you who your best future lamented was . . . Simply out of a wish to give you pleasure . . . Give me another."

Viktor got up and poured them both cognac, hands trembling visibly.

"You mean, *you* killed Yakornitsky?" He was aghast.

"Not me, *we*," corrected Misha. "But don't you worry, he more than had it coming . . . Another thing is that his death leaves out in the cold the privatization fanatics he milked of funds *on account*. Apart from that he retained certain documents touching on parliamentary colleagues by virtue of which he prolonged his own existence and security. It's a tough life they lead at the top . . . A kind of war."

A lengthy pause followed. Misha-non-penguin looked out of the window, leaving Viktor grappling with what he had been told.

"Listen," he said at last, "am I involved in the death of his mistress, too?"

"You haven't grasped it," said Misha in a calm, schoolteacher-like voice. "What you and I have done is pull out the bottommost card of the card house. Result: total collapse. Now we just wait for the dust to settle . . ."

"Me too?" Viktor asked, sounding alarmed.

Misha shrugged. "Individual matter," he said, replenishing his glass. "But you'll be all right. You, it seems, enjoy good protection . . . Which is why I've come to you."

"Whose?"

Misha gestured vaguely.

"I don't claim to know. Just a feeling. You wouldn't still be with us if you didn't." He became lost in thought. "Can I ask you to do me a favour?" he enquired after a while.

Viktor nodded.

"Go off to bed, and I'll sit on for a bit and have a think."

Viktor went to his room, lay down, but didn't feel like sleeping. He listened, but the silence of the flat was absolute. Everyone, it seemed, was sound asleep. Faintly from the living room came a child's voice. It was Sonya muttering *Mummy, Mummy*.

Who, he wondered, was where?

Eventually he dozed off.

A little later, the penguin emerged from behind the dark-green settee, and sauntered towards the half-open living-room door. En route he paused by the sleeping girl, gazed thoughtfully at her, then continued on into the corridor. Pushing the next door open, he proceeded to the kitchen.

Sitting asleep in his master's place, head resting on the table, was a strange man.

For several minutes the penguin considered him, standing motionless by the door, then turned about and retraced his steps.

24

The clock on the bedside table showed 7.00. Outside it was still dark and quiet. Having woken with a headache, Viktor lay on his back contemplating the ceiling and thinking about his conversation with Misha-non-penguin. Headache or no headache, he now had some questions for his caller of the night before.

Slowly, trying to make no sound, he got up, put on his dressing-gown, and went to the living room.

Sonya was still asleep, thoughtfully covered with Viktor's grey autumn overcoat from its hook in the hall.

Steeling himself, he went out into the corridor, only to be brought up short by the doors left open on the way to the kitchen.

The kitchen was empty. On the table was a note.

> Time to be off. Leaving Sonya with you. She's your responsibility – you answer for her with your life. Back when the dust settles. – Misha.

Caught unawares, Viktor sat at the table staring at the hand-written note, trying to put from his mind the questions he had intended to ask Misha-non-penguin, and hadn't.

Through the window, the grey of a wan winter dawn was contending with night.

His thoughts were interrupted by the creak of the living-room settee. Getting to his feet, he went and looked into the living room.

Sonya was sitting up, rubbing her eyes.

"Where's Daddy?" she asked, becoming aware of Viktor's presence.

"He's gone," he replied. "You're to live here for a bit."

"With Misha the penguin?" she asked brightly.

"Yes," he answered dryly.

"Yesterday we had our windows broken," she said. "And it was very cold."

"Your windows at home?"

"Yes," she confided. "Crash! Bang! they went. It was awful!"

"Like something to eat?"

"So long as it's not porridge."

"Haven't any," Viktor confessed. "I'm not a great eater."

"Me neither," said Sonya with a smile. "Where are we going today?"

"Where?" he repeated, trying to think. "I don't know . . . Where do you want to go?"

"The zoo."

"Right," he said, "but first I must do a couple of hours' work."

25

For lunch Viktor gave Misha fish, while he and Sonya had fried potatoes.

"I'll buy a bit more food tomorrow," he promised.

"This'll do me," she said, taking the larger plate.

Viktor smiled. Faced for the first time with another's childhood, he observed, cautiously, curiously, as though still a child himself. Sonya's spontaneity, her replies – not so much inopportune as somehow off at a tangent – brought a smile to his face. He ate with half an eye on her sitting opposite, eating more with interest than appetite, narrowly inspecting every forkful, while between her and the stove, Misha was busy at his bowl.

Once, she twisted round and transferred a fried potato to Misha's bowl on her fork. Head cocked comically to one side, Misha looked at her in surprise. Sonya burst out laughing. Misha stood for a while, then returned to his bowl and ate the fried potato.

"He likes it!" she reported, well pleased.

Viktor drank his tea, put Sonya into her coat, and they set off for the zoo.

It was snowing lightly, the wind in their faces, and coming out of the Metro he wrapped her up to the eyes in her scarf.

Beyond the gates there was a notice stating that owing to winter conditions only a small section of the zoo was open to visitors.

Not many people were about. Following a sign saying TIGERS, he led Sonya along a snow-covered path past an enclosure with a large drawing of a zebra and a stencilled description of its life and habits.

"Where," asked Sonya, looking around, "are the animals?"

"Further on," he said encouragingly.

They passed more empty enclosures with boards descriptive of recent inmates, and came to a roofed-in area.

Here, behind thick iron bars, sat two tigers, a lion, a wolf, and other predators. At the entrance there was a notice:

FEED ONLY WITH FRESH MEAT AND BREAD

Neither of which they had.

They walked along the cages, stopping briefly at each.

"Where," asked Sonya, "are the penguins?"

"Probably not in this part . . . Still, we'll come to them, if we keep looking."

He tried to remember exactly where he had first seen Misha. It

53

had been just beyond reptiles and amphibians and the concrete den for brown bears.

Walking on, they came to an empty sunken enclosure with railings around it and a frozen lake in the middle. A board depicting penguins hung above the railings.

"Well, as you can see, there aren't any here," said Viktor.

"A pity," sighed Sonya. "We could have brought Misha to make friends with the others."

"Except, as you can see, there aren't any others," he repeated, stooping down to her.

"What does still live here?" she asked.

For a whole hour more they wandered, seeing fish, snakes, two bald kites and a solitary long-necked llama. As they headed for the exit, Viktor spotted a sign:

SCIENTIFIC INFORMATION CENTRE

"Let's pop in," he suggested. "Maybe they can tell us about penguins."

"Yes, let's," Sonya agreed.

He knocked at the one door of the little single-storey building and went in.

"Excuse me," he said addressing a prematurely grey-haired woman sitting at a desk reading a periodical.

"Yes?" she said, looking up. "What can I do for you?"

"Just over a year ago," he said, "I took on one of your penguins. You don't happen to have anything about penguins, do you?"

"No. Pidpaly was penguins. Got fired when we gave them up. Took the literature with him. Noxious old man."

"Pidpaly, you say? Where can I find him?"

"Try Personnel," she shrugged, and looking with interest at

Sonya, asked, "You couldn't, I suppose, do with the odd snake? Reptiles and amphibians go from January."

"Thank you, no. Where is Personnel?"

"Back of toilets, left of main entrance."

Leaving Sonya to wait at the entrance, Viktor went and obtained Pidpaly's address. Folding the piece of paper, he put it into his wallet, took her hand, and they set off for the Metro.

26

Next morning he decided to go and see the Chief. Firstly, because he had a backlog of copy to deliver, and secondly, out of a desire to confess – or rather explain – what had happened to Yakornitsky – and why.

"Could you stay here alone?" he asked Sonya after breakfast.

"Daddy told me," she said. "*Let no one in. Don't answer the phone. Keep away from windows.* That right?"

"Yes," sighed Viktor. "But today you can go to the windows."

"Can I?" she said happily, running to the balcony door and pressing her nose to the pane.

"And what can you see?"

"Winter."

"Back soon," promised Viktor.

He had to show his Press card three times before arriving at the Chief's office.

"How are we?" enquired Igor Lvovich.

"Fine," said Viktor without conviction. "I've brought you these new *obelisks*."

The Chief reached out a hand. "And this," he passed over a fat folder, "is from Fyodor."

"Igor," Viktor began, plucking up courage. "It seems it's me who's actually to blame for Yakornitsky's death."

"You don't say!" grinned the Chief. "See yourself as a heavy, do you?"

Viktor looked bewildered.

"No need to fret," said the Chief in a more amicable tone. "I know everything."

"Everything?"

"Considerably more than everything. Yakornitsky had the skids under him anyway . . . So don't worry! Though you would do better to stick to what concerns you, of course."

Viktor stared aghast, unable to take it all in.

"So it's not the end of the world," he said at last.

"Why should it be? Just because we're one little group with government connections the fewer? Relax. You're out of it, and if you're not, you're only very indirectly in. Let's have some coffee."

The Chief phoned the order to his secretary, then looked hard at Viktor, thoughtfully biting his lip.

"No wife? No girlfriend?"

"Not at the moment."

"Bad," said the Chief with a half-humorous shake of the head. "Women are the strength of the male nervous system. Time you took your nerves in hand . . . Still, just my little joke."

The secretary brought coffee.

Viktor took half a spoonful of sugar, but the overstrong coffee was still bitter, making him think of his recent trip to Kharkov.

"Do I have to go to Odessa?" he asked suddenly, remembering their pre-Kharkov conversation.

"No," replied the Chief. "Someone's very much anti our getting involved in the provinces . . . Still, we've enough to be getting on with here. So no need to worry. Look at me, serene as a tank, even though they've just murdered my driver! Believe me, life's not something to be concerned about."

Seeing the Chief in his expensive suit, French tie, solid gold tie-pin, and director's chair, Viktor doubted whether he did, in fact, set so little store by life.

"Before New Year we must split a bottle together, you and I, eh? Unless you'd rather not?"

"All for it," answered Viktor.

"Good." The Chief got to his feet. "I'll be in touch."

27

Stepan Yakovlevich Pidpaly lived on the ground floor of a grey Stalin-baroque block near Svyatoshino Metro station. Stamping the snow off his feet, Viktor rang the bell.

Lengthy spyhole scrutiny followed, then a trembly old man's voice asked, "Who do you want?"

"Stepan Yakovlevich," said Viktor.

"Who are you?"

"I got your address at the zoo," explained Viktor. "I've come about penguins."

The apparent idiocy of this explanation notwithstanding, the door opened, and an unshaven, not so very old-looking man in a blue woollen tracksuit invited him in.

He went through into a spacious living room in the middle

of which was an old-fashioned round table with chairs.

"Sit down," said his host, looking elsewhere.

"Interested in penguins, are you?" he went on, now looking squarely at Viktor, at the same time feeling for and retrieving an old dog-end from the grubby table cloth. The hand descended below the table then came up without the dog-end, and rested on the cloth.

"I'm sorry to trouble you," began Viktor, "but I wanted to ask if maybe you had any books on penguins."

"Books?" Pidpaly countered, looking pained. "Why should I? I've got my own unpublished works . . . I've studied penguins for more than 20 years."

"So you're a zoologist?" said Viktor as deferentially as he knew how.

"*Penguinologist*, more like, though it's not a speciality you'll find listed, of course." His tone softened. "Still, what's your interest in penguins exactly?"

"I have one, but know nothing about them. I'm worried in case I'm doing something wrong."

"You have, have you? Splendid! Where did you get him?"

"From the zoo, a year ago. When smaller animals were being given away."

Pidpaly frowned. "What species?"

"King, I think. Called Misha. Fully grown, about as tall as this table."

"*Misha!*" Pidpaly pursed his lips, scratched his stubble. "From our zoo?"

"Yes."

"Well I never! But why take on a sick one? There were seven of them, I remember. Adèle, Zaychik – they were the younger, fit ones."

58

"What's wrong with him?"

"Depressive syndrome. Bad heart. I'd say congenital. So *that's* where he got to," he said sadly with a sigh.

"What can be done about it? Can he be treated?"

"That's a good one!" Pidpaly laughed. "They don't treat people nowadays, let alone penguins! What you must realize is that our climate's fatal to creatures from the Antarctic. The best thing for him, of course, would be to be living where he belongs. You mustn't take it amiss, and I'm clearly talking rubbish, but if I were a penguin and found myself in these latitudes, I'd do myself in. Imagine the torment of living where it's up to 40°+ in summer and *occasionally* down to -10° in winter, when you've got two layers of fat protecting you against intense cold, to say nothing of hundreds of blood vessels doing the same. Just imagine: you get superheated internally. You burn up . . . Practically all penguins living in zoos exhibit depressive syndrome . . . And they tried to tell me penguins had no psychology. I proved it! And I'll prove it to you! And as to his heart: what heart *would* tolerate superheating to that extent?"

As Viktor listened, Pidpaly became more and more worked up, and waved his arms about ever more wildly. From time to time he switched to rhetorical questions, pausing briefly to catch breath before continuing. Never had Viktor received such an earful: period of incubation . . . physiology . . . mating peculiarities . . . Eventually, with a headache coming on, he knew he must somehow arrest the flow.

"Excuse me, but may I read what you've written?" he interposed, exploiting one of Pidpaly's periodic rhetorical questions. "On penguins, I mean."

"Of course," said Pidpaly slowly. "As long as I get it back."

Going into the next room – which, seen through the open door, was clearly a study – he bent over a great writing desk and rummaged in one of the drawers. At long last he straightened up and came back with a fat loose-leaf file.

"Here we are," he said, putting it down on the table. "It won't all be of interest, of course, but if some of it is, I'll be happy."

"May I perhaps do something in return?" asked Viktor, anxious to show appreciation, but uncertain how.

"Yes," confided the penguinologist quietly, "what you could do, when you return my manuscript, is bring a couple of kilograms of potatoes."

28

Two weeks passed. Sonya grew accustomed to the new flat and asked less often about Daddy. Viktor became accustomed to Sonya, as he had earlier to Misha. But he often thought of her father, having no idea what was happening to him, or even if he was still alive.

The window looked out on winter. Some evenings, when it was dark and not many people were about, he took Sonya and Misha for a walk. They strolled the waste area by the three dovecotes, snow crunching beneath their feet. Sometimes stray mongrels came running up to Misha, and instead of barking, sniffed this strange, unresponsive creature in silence. Waving her arms and puffing out her cheeks, Sonya would rush at them and off they would run, leaving her happy.

Viktor had read the whole of Pidpaly's manuscript. A lot of

it was beyond him, but he had still discovered useful things. He made a note of the most important pages and had them photocopied at the nearest bookshop, after which he put the manuscript in a prominent place in the kitchen, to be returned in the near future.

Work was also advancing. The folder he had received from the Chief had been duly processed, and twelve new *obelisks* lay on the window ledge awaiting their appointed hour. They had given him trouble, the Chief's underlinings having proved too extensive for the *obelisk* as elaborated and perfected by Viktor. It had meant altering the rhythm, adding pace, and presenting the underlinings as brief biographical inserts, which made them look more like quotes from an indictment.

With this batch completed, he was struck for the first time by the thought that only one of his obituaries – an unplanned one – had had as subject an unsullied victim, with no fact or hint suggestive of a dubious past. Yuliya Parkhomenko, the singer, was who he had in mind. But now he had his doubts. He recalled the allusion to involvement in the disappearance of another artiste . . . And her love for the late Yakornitsky . . . No. The pure and sinless did not exist, or else died unnoticed and with no obituary. The idea seemed persuasive. Those who merited obituaries had usually achieved things, fought for their ideals, and when locked in battle, it wasn't easy to remain entirely honest and upright. Today's battles were all for material gain, anyway. The crazy idealist was extinct – survived by the crazy pragmatist . . .

District Militiaman Sergey had phoned a number of times, and the previous Sunday they had been for another picnic on the Dnieper ice, only now with Sonya. A pleasant time had been had by all. Misha swam to his heart's content in the broad ice-hole. Viktor and Sergey drank cognac-laced coffee, lying on the same quilted blanket. Sonya had the Pepsi Cola and sweets that had been bought for her. And all three watched the ice-hole from which Misha would leap as if bitten, becoming airborne for a metre or so before landing, comically, on the ice, and hurrying back to the blanket. Sonya would towel him solicitously, and he would then comically pick his way back to the hole.

They sat there almost till dusk, then had to hurry across the grey-blue ice of the frozen Dnieper to the *Zaporozhets*, parked as before, by the lower Monastery Gardens.

After which the week began again as usual, except that Viktor was conscious of additional concerns now that he was responsible for Sonya, and they began to eat better as a consequence. He took to buying German fruit yogurts and fresh vegetables, and the penguin's fare included frozen shrimps, which he relished.

"Why haven't you got a telly?" Sonya asked one day. "Don't you like cartoons?"

"No, I don't," said Viktor.

"I do," the little girl answered gravely.

New Year approached. Trees decorated with toys appeared in the shops. In Kreshchatik Street they were assembling the National Tree from smaller firs. People were looking more relaxed, and the papers contained hardly anything about shootings or bomb blasts. It was as if the whole of Kiev, regardless of profession, was on holiday.

Viktor had already bought Sonya's New Year present and hidden it in a cupboard. It was a Barbie doll. Together they selected a little fir tree with a base, took it back to the flat and decorated it with ribbons and old toys found in the attic.

"Do you believe in Grandfather Frost?" he asked once.

"Yes," she said in surprise, "don't you?"

"Yes," said Viktor.

"Wait for New Year – he's bound to bring you something," she promised.

29

Leaving Sonya at the flat, Viktor shopped at the food store, and travelled out to Pidpaly's.

Again it was a blue-tracksuited Pidpaly who came to the door, and he was barefoot.

"All for me?" he asked, delightedly examining Viktor's edible gifts. "You really shouldn't have."

At the bottom of the bag, under all the purchases, was the penguinologist's file, which Viktor handed back with thanks.

"Any use to you?"

"A great help."

"Sit down. I'll make some tea," said Pidpaly, bustling about.

It turned out to be green. Pidpaly passed it to him in a bowl, setting down a little box of chipped sugar of heaven alone knew what provenance, such as Viktor had seen only in old films.

Snapping off a piece, he washed it down with the tea, and took a sly look at the little box.

"Doesn't spoil, you see," said Pidpaly, following the direction of his gaze. "Ages back I bought three loaves, and I've still got some . . . Time was, there was more shape, more taste to things. Remember Capital Meat Loaf?"

Viktor shook his head.

"Missed out on the time of abundance, you have," said the old man regretfully. "Every century there's five years of abundance, after which everything goes to pot . . . You won't see the next five, I'm afraid – I certainly won't. But I did at least come in for one lot. How's the penguin?"

"Fine," said Viktor. "You remember you mentioned penguin psychology."

"I do indeed."

"Just how much do they understand?"

"They're quick to distinguish mood – in people and other animals, of course. Apart from that, they're very unforgiving. They've also a good memory for anything good. But their psychology, you understand, is far more complex than, say, a dog or a cat's. They're more intelligent, more secretive; capable of concealing feelings and affections."

Having drunk his tea, Viktor jotted down his telephone number on a piece of paper.

"If you want anything, ring," he said, handing it to the penguinologist.

"Thank you, thank you. And you ring, too, and come and see me."

As the old man got up, Viktor again noticed that his feet were bare.

"Won't you catch cold?" he asked.

"No," Pidpaly assured him. "I do yoga. I've a book with photographs – all Indian yogis go barefoot."

"Only because India has no winter, and shoes are expensive," Viktor said, letting himself out. "Goodbye."

"Happy New Year!" called Pidpaly after his departing visitor.

30

Waking very early a few days before New Year, Viktor noticed three large brightly wrapped parcels under the tree in the living room. He looked in at Sonya. She was still asleep.

Who had put them there? Sonya or Grandfather Frost?

He washed, went to the kitchen, and there on the table was an envelope.

This, on top of an uneasy night's sleep, was the limit.

He remembered dreaming he had been hiding from someone at dead of night in a strange flat, listening tensely to a silence occasionally broken by faint footsteps and the squeaking of doors. The envelope was sealed. He cut off one end with scissors, and clearly written in block-capitals, read:

HAPPY NEW YEAR! MY THANKS FOR SONYA. HER PRESENTS AND YOURS ARE UNDER THE TREE. NAMESAKE'S PRESENT IS IN THE FREEZER. HOPING NEW YEAR WILL BRING YOU SOME RELIEF. SORRY I CAN'T POP IN . . .

TILL THEN — MISHA.

Viktor looked around, bewildered, as if expecting to see who had brought it.

He went and tried the door. It was, as usual, double-locked on the inside.

Shrugging, he returned to the kitchen. What had occurred was as inexplicable as it was blatant, and left him totally perplexed. His locks no longer protected him, whether sleeping or awake, and in case of danger would be useless.

He was not so much alarmed as amazed.

Outside, cottony snow was gliding down at an angle to the wind.

31

When Sonya woke, she was delighted to find presents under the tree.

"You see!" she said. "Grandfather Frost! He could come again."

Viktor gave a knowing smile.

After breakfast Sonya wanted to open her presents, but he stopped her.

"Mine's there too," he said, squatting down in front of her, "but it's only the 29th! Two more days to go!"

Reluctantly she agreed to wait.

While Sonya busied herself telling Misha a fairy story in the bedroom, Viktor made coffee, then sat, cup in hand, at the table facing the window.

The year that was ending had brought much that was strange into his life. And it was ending strangely, engendering mixed feelings and thoughts. Loneliness had given way to a kind of semi-loneliness, a kind of semi-dependence. His own sluggish life force had borne him as on a wave to a strange island, where suddenly he had acquired responsibilities and money to discharge them. Remaining, in the process, remote from events and even from life itself, he had made no effort to grasp what was taking place around him. Until recently, with the arrival of Sonya. And even now, life around him was still dangerously unfathomable, as if he had missed the actual moment when the nature of events might have been fathomed.

His world was now him, Penguin Misha and Sonya, but so vulnerable did it seem, this little world, that should anything happen, it would be beyond his power to protect it. Not for lack of a weapon or karate skills, but simply because, containing no genuine attachment, no sense of unity, no woman, it was too ready to crumble. Sonya was someone else's little girl temporarily in his care, his penguin was sickly and sad, and under no obligation to show gratitude doggy-fashion, wagging his tail after fresh-frozen fish.

His reflections interrupted by the phone, he went back to the living room to answer it.

It was the Chief.

"Coming round for half an hour. All right?"

"Fine," said Viktor.

He peeped into the bedroom. Sonya and the penguin were standing facing each other.

"Have you understood what I've said?" she was asking, and her tone was insistent.

They were, he now saw, much the same height.

"Very well," said Sonya, "and then I'll make you a new suit in quite a different colour . . ."

Smiling, he tiptoed away. An hour later the Chief arrived, and spent a long time shaking snow from his long overcoat before finally coming in.

"Happy New Year!" he said, putting down a heavy carrier bag.

They went through into the kitchen, where Igor Lvovich pulled from his bag a bottle of champagne, a lemon, a couple of tins and several packages.

He called for a cutting board and knives, and together they sliced sausage, cheese and baguette. After which Viktor fetched glasses.

"Got a cat, have you?" the Chief asked, noting the fish head in the bowl on the little bedside table by the stove.

"No, a penguin."

He laughed. "You're joking!"

"I'm not. Come and see."

Viktor took him to the bedroom.

"And who's this then?" asked the Chief, seeing the little girl. "Didn't you say you weren't married?"

"It's Sonya!" she said, eyeing the strange uncle. "And this," she said, pointing at the penguin, "is Misha."

"Daughter of a friend," murmured Viktor so that Sonya shouldn't hear.

The Chief inclined his head.

"Pity I didn't know about the penguin," he said, back in the kitchen. "My youngest has only seen them in books."

"Bring him another time."

"Another time?" the Chief repeated thoughtfully. "Yes, of course. This year he's been with my wife in Italy. It's quieter there."

Head back, gaze directed at the ceiling, the Chief restrained the cork from flying there, and poured champagne.

"Happy New Year!" he said.

Viktor raised his glass. "Happy New Year!"

"Where are you seeing it in?" the Chief asked after a gulp of champagne.

"Here."

Prodding his fork into the salami, the Chief nodded, shooting Viktor another of his looks, this time one of concern.

"You see," he said, "I've got some rather unseasonable news for you . . . But it's the way it's turned out."

Viktor looked at him intently.

"They're on to you. They're pumping people in my office as

68

to who our *obelisk* writer is. It's good that no one knows, apart from Fyodor and me."

"What are they on to me for?" Viktor asked, putting down his champagne half drunk.

"The fact is," the Chief said hesitantly, carefully choosing his words, "that you, Viktor, have done us proud . . . Getting in all my underlinings, I mean. In actual fact, each obituary, apart from mentioning the late lamented's sins, has hinted where those advantaged by his death are to be looked for. Evidently someone's guessed what the game is – that they're simply being set on collision courses. Still, we've achieved quite a lot. And we'll do better. We'll just have to change tactics."

"*We*? The paper, you mean?" asked Viktor, utterly dismayed, trying to remember where he had heard about *collision courses* before.

"Not just us," the Chief said gently. "And not so much us as a paper even, but as a body of people endeavouring to clean this country up a bit . . . Don't worry, though – our security's on to whoever's on to you. But to give time for our boys to cope, you'll need to lie low for a while."

"When?" Viktor asked, flabbergasted.

"The sooner the better," came the calm reply.

Viktor sat at the table, a picture of dejection.

"Nothing to be afraid of. Fear's dangerous," said Igor Lvovich. "Best be thinking where to lie low . . . And don't tell me. Just give the odd ring. OK?"

Viktor nodded mechanically.

"And now let's drink to all going well at my end," said the Chief topping up their glasses. "If it does, *you* won't be the loser, I promise."

Reluctantly Viktor raised his glass.

"Drink up!" urged the Chief. "There's no escaping fate. Drink while the champagne lasts!"

Viktor took a gulp, and almost choked as bubbles of gas prickled his nose.

"I wouldn't be here now, if I didn't value you highly," Igor Lvovich said, preparing to leave and donning his long dark-green overcoat. "Ring in a week or so. No work for the time being, so you find some nice secluded spot and lie doggo."

The door banged. The Chief's footsteps died away, leaving Viktor to an uneasy silence and musings much inhibited by the champagne he had drunk. He stood staring at the closed door, trying again to solve the riddle of the nocturnal Grandfather Frost who had brought news and presents from Misha-non-penguin.

"Uncle Vik!" called Sonya from the living room. "Uncle Vik! He knocked me over!"

Returning to the present, he quickly went to her.

"What happened?" he asked, looking down at her lying on the floor.

"Nothing," she said, with a guilty smile.

Beside her stood Misha, *regardant*.

"I was trying to see what your present was, and he knocked me over," she confessed at last. "I wasn't looking at mine. Just taking a peep at yours."

"Up you get," said Viktor, giving her his hand.

Sonya got to her feet.

"Can I go for a walk?"

"No," he snapped.

"Just a teeny-weeny one."

But why not? There were plenty of children around.

"All right, but not for long, and don't go away from the block."

Having put her into her fur coat and muffled her up to her eyes in her scarf, he let Sonya go, settled himself at the kitchen table, and became lost in thought. With every day bringing far from pleasant surprises, he had plenty to ponder.

32

He was seized with sudden panic. He was still sitting at the table, the champagne finished, the sausage eaten, the slight feeling of intoxication gone. His head was clear, his legs steady.

He looked out of the window. The snow had eased enough for him to see, down below, several children from the block busy building a snow castle.

Standing on the little bedside table, he stuck his head out of the small vent and shouted, "Sonya! Home! Quick!"

The children looked up from building their castle, but they all stayed standing where they were.

Hard as he stared, he couldn't see Sonya among them. Quickly putting on his sheepskin coat and fur hat, he dashed from the flat. Spotting some other children a short distance from the block, he ran towards them, but there was no Sonya.

Hearing an engine start up behind him, he swung round. An old Mercedes was moving off from the block opposite. Something prompted him to give chase. Managing by some miracle not to fall, he caught it up at the turning before the exit to the road, but here, feet skidding beneath him, he fell forward onto the boot, to the consternation of the driver, the sole occupant of the car. Picking himself up, Viktor walked back to the block.

He had been foolish to let her go out, after what the Chief had said.

At the top of the stairs, he found her leaning against the door of the flat.

"Where have you been?" he shouted.

"At Anya's, on the ground floor," she said guiltily. "She was showing me her Sindy doll."

He ought to punish her in some way, he thought, but gradually he grew calmer.

"Like something to eat?" he asked.

"Has Misha eaten?"

"No."

"Then we can eat together," she said happily.

33

After supper Viktor rang Sergey Fischbein-Stepanenko, asking him to come as soon as he could. He did, and they shut themselves in the kitchen, leaving Sonya and Misha in the living room.

Viktor thought first of inventing some cover story for Sergey's benefit, but in the end saw the stupidity of doing so. Why, when needing help, bring in deceit? The account he gave, if lacking in coherence, found Sergey quick on the uptake.

"I've got a dacha," he said. "One of an MVD group. There's a public phone, a fireplace and a TV, and food in the cellar . . . Why not celebrate New Year there?"

"But where were you planning to celebrate it?" Viktor asked cautiously.

Sergey shrugged. "Nowhere," he said. "You know the extent of my intimate circle."

"And your mother?"

"Won't have anything to do with New Year. Doesn't like festive occasions. When would you like to go?"

"The sooner the better. Today?"

Sergey looked out of the window. It was getting dark.

"Right, but I must pop home first as I haven't got the keys with me." He rose from the table. "Back in an hour. You get your things together."

After seeing him out, Viktor looked into the living room.

"Sonya," he said, squatting down in front of her, "we're going away."

"When do we come back?"

"In a few days."

"What if Grandfather Frost comes and we're not here?"

"He's got keys," said Viktor. "He'll leave his presents under the tree."

"Will there be a tree where we're going?"

Viktor shook his head.

"Then I shan't go," she declared firmly.

He sighed a deep sigh.

"Listen," he said sternly. "When Daddy comes back, I shall tell him how naughty you've been."

"And I shall tell him you don't read to me, or buy me ice-creams," vowed Sonya.

Finding the reproach justified, Viktor fell silent.

"OK," he said after a while. "You're absolutely right. But

73

we're expected. We can take our tree with us, if you like."

"Is Misha coming?"

"Of course."

"OK."

Together they removed the decorations and toys from the tree, and wrapped them in paper.

"We'll take the presents, too," Sonya insisted, and obediently Viktor put them into a shopping bag.

"Wait," she said, suddenly stopping. "What if Grandfather Frost comes and there's no tree, where will he put his presents?"

He was at a loss. No sensible answer suggested itself. He felt infinitely weary.

"Perhaps we should paint a fir tree on the wall to tell him where," said Sonya, pondering the matter aloud. "Got any green paint?"

"No," said Viktor. "I know what – we'll leave a note in the kitchen saying put them on the table."

Sonya thought.

"*Under* is better."

"Why?"

"So nobody sees."

That settled, Viktor wrote the note. Sonya read it syllable by syllable, and gave it back with a nod of approval.

Down below a car hooted. Viktor looked out, and in the late afternoon gloom, was just able to make out the familiar *Zaporozhets*.

First he carried down the tree, trussed in washing-line, together with a shopping bag of toys and presents, and a carrier bag of food from the freezer; then he and Sonya went down, he with Misha in his arms.

"I've brought a couple more blankets," said Sergey in the car. "Until the place heats up, it'll be cold."

Misha and Sonya sat at the back, Viktor in front. Misha edged closer to Sonya when the engine started, as if scared by the noise. Seeing them in the mirror snuggled up together, Viktor nudged Sergey and pointed. Adjusting the mirror to this amusing rear-seat idyll, Sergey gave a weary smile and accelerated away.

34

At the entrance to the dacha plots was a hut from which two men in camouflaged combat gear emerged, walked around the *Zaporozhets*, and took a good look inside. Sergey wound down the window.

"Dacha 7."

"Carry on," said one of the guards.

They stopped outside a little brick-built house with a steeply angled roof. Sergey got out. Looking into the back before following, Viktor saw that Sonya was asleep.

"Just a mo while I unset the trap," said Sergey.

"What trap?"

"Anti-burglar."

Stooping, and with a creaking of boards, he shifted something in front of the door.

"All's well," he beckoned. "We can enter."

Opening the door to a glassed-in veranda, Sergey switched on the light, throwing a yellow pool onto the snow in front of the house and the car. Sonya woke, rubbed her eyes, and turned to Misha, around whom she had had her arm for the whole of the journey. Sensing she was awake, he turned towards her and they looked hard at one another.

In no time they were all sitting in a cold room before a dead hearth, with a single bulb dispensing light and an illusion of warmth from the ceiling.

Sergey brought wood, built it into a wigwam in the hearth, and inserted a lighted newspaper.

The flames took hold, and slowly began to radiate heat.

Misha, who had tucked himself away in a far corner, suddenly livened up and came and stood in front of the fire.

"Uncle Vik," yawned Sonya, "when are we going to see to the tree?"

"Tomorrow morning," said Viktor.

The small room contained a settee and an armchair facing the fire, and against the left-hand wall, a bed.

They put Sonya on the settee close to the fire with the two blankets over her, and she soon fell asleep, leaving Viktor, Sergey and Misha to keep vigil by the blazing hearth. Sergey added more wood. Apart from the occasional hiss of moisture issuing from the logs, there wasn't a sound.

Viktor perched on the edge of the settee, Sergey sat in the armchair, and Misha, not taught by nature how to sit, stood.

"I'm off to work tomorrow," said Sergey. "I'll get champagne and some meat afterwards and come back."

Viktor nodded.

"It's so quiet here," he said dreamily. "A silence to sit and write in."

"No one's stopping you," Sergey said amiably.

"Life is," said Viktor, after a silence.

"It is you who's made it complicated . . . Let's have a smoke on the veranda."

Viktor went, though he didn't smoke. After the slightly warmed air of the living room, the veranda was like a refrigerator, but invigorating.

Sergey exhaled a stream of smoke towards the low ceiling. "Look," he said, "if you're in that sort of a mess, why drag a small girl around with you?"

"Her father seems to be in the same boat. I've no idea where he is. So what can I do?"

Sergey shrugged. "Ah, we're not alone," he said a minute later, looking out of the window.

Two windows were shining bright in the darkness.

"Like some cherry brandy?" Sergey asked suddenly.

"Rather!"

"They went through to the tiny ice-cold kitchen, where there was just a stand with an electric hotplate and a small table with two stools. Sergey raised a rectangle of wooden floor and thrust a torch at Viktor.

"Light me down," he told him, and Viktor obeyed.

Lowering himself into the cellar, Sergey passed up two old champagne bottles corked with babies' dummies, then climbed back up.

They sat straight down in the kitchen, filled cut-glass tumblers with cherry brandy, and drank in leisurely fashion, listening to the silence. Sergey went to put more wood on the fire.

"Is she asleep?" Viktor asked when he returned.

"Yes."

"And Misha?

"Keeping an eye on the fire," Sergey grinned. "Well, shall we drink to the New Year?"

With a sigh Viktor grasped his glass. That, too, was cold.

"As a butcher friend of mine was wont to say," continued Sergey, "*Let's drink to not being worse off. We have known better days.*"

35

Next morning Sergey left for Kiev, and Viktor filled a bucket from the water pipe running overground through the plots. After putting the kettle on the electric hotplate, he looked into the living room. The fire had burnt itself out in the night, but warmth and a scent of pine remained. Sonya was asleep and smiling. Misha stood brooding over the heap of black ash in the hearth.

Viktor slapped his thigh, and as Misha turned, half opened the door and beckoned.

"Come," he whispered.

With a backward look at the dead hearth, Misha came waddling.

"Hungry? Of course you are. Come on, let's go out."

From the shopping bag he took a couple of plaice, which he laid on the top step.

"Tuck in!"

Misha came out onto the step, and swivelled his head left and right, taking in his surroundings. Descending to the snow, he marched around in a circle and headed towards the trees, but coming up against the water pipe, turned back, his tracks not unlike those of crooked skis, describing irregular geometric figures on the clean page of snow. Returning, he edged round the steps, and treating the topmost as a table, addressed himself to the fish.

Well pleased at such a display of animation, Viktor proceeded to the kitchen and made tea. He looked into the living room. Sonya was still sleeping and he didn't want to wake her.

He sat with his cup of tea at the kitchen table. On the window ledge beside him stood the two bottles of cherry brandy, one half empty, the other full. Romantic thoughts stirred in the silence, touching again on unwritten novels and the past. He suddenly had the sensation of being abroad, out of reach of yesterday's existence. This abroad was a place of tranquillity, a Switzerland of the soul blanketed in snows of peace, permeated with a dread of causing disturbance; where no bird sang or called, as if out of no desire to.

At a sound from the veranda door, he went to investigate, and came face to face with Misha, who, seeing Viktor, comically bowed his head, giving him to understand that he liked it here. Ample food and suitably cold, Viktor decided, pleased at his friend's good spirits.

Soon after, Sonya woke, putting an end to silence and reflection. First he must give her breakfast, then get to work on the tree.

The tree took more than an hour, but finally there it stood, decked with ribbons and toys, in trampled snow and less than lofty splendour, with Misha beside it, keeping an eye on events.

Sonya walked back to see how it looked from the dacha.

"Like it?"

"Yes!" she said, delighted.

They made a tour of the little garden, then went back in. Viktor re-lit the fire, and Sonya settled down in the armchair with a pencil and an exercise book she had found.

Towards five, when it was dark and the room was warm, suffused with the yellow light of the single ceiling bulb, Sergey returned. He dumped two shopping bags on the veranda, then parked his car behind the dacha.

"Brought you the latest," he said, handing Viktor a bundle of newspapers. "I've got a couple of bottles of champagne and one of pepper vodka – in case of colds. Will that be enough?"

"Ample," said Viktor, opening out the first of the papers.

BANKER MURDERED

ATTEMPTED ASSASSINATION OF STATE DEPUTY

The headlines jolted him back to reality. Skimming both articles, he tried to think. The banker's name rang no bell. *He was not obelisk*-carded. The State Deputy – *only wounded*, albeit in the head – *was*.

"Look, old friend," said Sergey, "I didn't bring these to furrow your brow!"

Viktor let the papers slide to the floor by the hearth. "They'll do for fire-lighting," he said.

"Quite right! News you can't read calmly, don't read at all!" said Sergey. Then, turning to Sonya in her armchair, he asked, "And what are you up to?"

"Drawing a stove."

"Show me."

He studied the drawing in the exercise book, and turned to her with a puzzled expression.

"Why's the fire black?"

"It's not, it's grey," she corrected. "Because I only found one pencil."

"Didn't look hard enough," said Sergey. "OK, tomorrow we'll both look. There must be others – my niece brought some."

They fried potatoes, made a good supper, then settled Sonya for the night.

"I shan't sleep," she warned. "I shall watch the fire, and if it goes out, I'll call."

Leaving it at that, they sat at the kitchen table and retrieved yesterday's cut-glass tumblers from the window ledge. Sergey filled them, and dropped the empty bottle on the floor.

"One more day, and that's it," said Sergey. "Then back to the same old thing, except that the year will be new."

At two in the morning they were still sitting, hotplate glowing red for warmth. Though the second bottle was empty, they felt unjustifiably sober. Only indolence kept Sergey from the second visit to the cellar that seemed highly desirable.

Suddenly an explosion set the windows rattling and made them start up in alarm.

"Shall we go and see?" Viktor asked uncertainly.

Sergey looked into the living room. Sonya was muttering in her sleep. The fire was burning low.

"Yes," he said, returning to the kitchen. Standing on the top step they found Misha.

"Seems to be asleep," whispered Viktor, after bending to look.

Voices broke the silence. Words couldn't be distinguished, but the intonation was one of alarm. Snow crunched beneath the feet of people invisible in the darkness. The cones of light shed by solitary lamps at 100-metre intervals along the main avenue had merely the effect of provoking the darkness into closing in more impenetrably.

"Come on," called Sergey, now more decisive.

"But where?"

"Not far."

Coming to one of the footpaths that served to delimit the plots, they followed it for 100 metres or so, before stopping and listening.

"Over there!" Sergey pointed in the direction of voices made louder by the silence of the night.

As they made their way towards the voices, they saw the beam of a powerful torch moving slowly over the snow.

"Local man," they heard a wheezy voice declare.

"That's Grandpa Vanya, dacha caretaker," Sergey whispered.

Advancing, they made themselves known.

"What's up, Vanya?" Sergey enquired.

"The old story," said the caretaker, directing the beam of his massive accumulator-powered torch at a body lying on the snow. The snow, Viktor saw, was red, and the body minus a leg and an arm. The latter, torn off at the elbow, lay some distance away, still in its padded sleeve.

Two men, one tall and wearing a tracksuit, the other slightly shorter, bearded and wearing a down jacket, were standing there saying nothing.

Someone could be heard running, stamping down the snow as he came, and a man dressed in camouflage combat gear and holding an automatic pistol came over to them and halted, breathing hard.

"What's up?" he panted.

"This," said the caretaker, directing the beam of his torch at the body lying face down in the snow. "Local man. Out stealing. Trod on a mine."

"Ah," said Camouflage Suit, putting away his weapon. "Killed in furtherance of attempted burglary."

A dog burst suddenly out of the darkness, darted, tail wagging, around the caretaker's legs, went and sniffed the corpse, then, snatching up the arm in its jaws, raced away into the darkness.

"Druzhok! Stop, damn you!" shouted the caretaker, but as the echo played back his hoarseness, he fell silent.

"Do we report it?" asked Camouflage Suit.

"What the hell for?" asked Down Jacket with Beard. "We didn't come to have our holiday messed up giving evidence!"

"So what do we do?" the caretaker asked of no one in particular.

"Cover him with snow, tramp it down, and leave him till after the holiday," Camouflage Suit suggested, after a moment's thought.

As his leg was jabbed suddenly from behind, Viktor started forward, thinking it to be Druzhok returned from burying tomorrow's breakfast, but it was Misha.

Viktor squatted down in front of him. "How did you get here?" he asked. "I thought you were asleep."

"Whatever have you got there?" Camouflage Suit asked coming over. "Not a penguin? Hell's bells! So you have!"

"Ruddy marvel!" laughed the man in the tracksuit. "Ruddy marvel!"

In next to no time, all were crowded round Misha, the corpse in the snow forgotten.

"Is he tame?" asked Down Jacket with Beard.

"Not very," said Viktor.

"What do you call him?" asked the caretaker.

"Misha."

"Ah, Misha, little Misha," coaxed the caretaker hoarsely. Then, turning to those assembled, said, "All right, off you go.

And if there's a bottle in it, I'll cover him over."

"There will be," Down Jacket with Beard promised. "Pop in first thing tomorrow."

Viktor, Sergey and Misha followed the boundary footpath back.

"Are all the dachas here mined?" Viktor asked.

"Not all," replied Sergey. "I've got a different, more humane sort of trap."

"What sort?"

"Ship's siren. Wake every village around, that would!"

The snow crunched under their feet. Cold stars pierced the clear, immeasurably deep sky. There was no moon and the night seemed the darker for it.

"Here we are then." Sergey stopped at the steps and looked round at Viktor and the penguin who were following. "Ah, you've decorated the tree!" he said in surprise. "I missed that when I drove in. Well done!"

The veranda door creaked, after which silence fell once more over the dacha plots.

The room was warm. Ash glowed in the hearth. Sonya was sleeping and smiling.

Not feeling sleepy, Viktor and Sergey shut themselves in the kitchen again.

36

Next morning Sergey and Viktor devoted themselves to preparations for New Year. The first thing was to bring the ancient television down from its hiding place in the loft. They put it in the warm living room, plugged it in and got it working. As good luck would have it, cartoons were showing, and Sonya settled herself in the armchair to watch.

From the cellar they brought up a three-litre jar of cucumbers, tomatoes and peppers, jointly pickled, two more bottles of cherry brandy and a couple of kilos of potatoes.

"What we have to do now," said Sergey, rubbing his palms together with satisfaction, "is see to the meat and get wood for the bonfire."

Time dragged, as if the year was no longer in a hurry to depart.

When the meat had been cut up and left to marinate, wood chopped and built into a nice little stack near the tree, and other minor tasks completed, it was still only midday by the clock.

It was sunny and frosty. Misha stood on the top step watching a tiny flock of bullfinches wandering over the snow.

"How about a glass?" Sergey suggested, and sitting down at the kitchen table, they poured themselves cherry brandy.

"To time – and may it fly," proposed Sergey, clinking glasses with Viktor.

The toast did the trick, and time did go a little faster. After lunch all save the penguin lay down for a rest, and even Sonya made no objection to Sergey's switching off the TV and declaring a quiet hour.

When they woke, it was dark and the clock said 5.30.

"That was a good sleep!" said Sergey, stepping outside and rubbing his somewhat puffy face with snow to freshen up, as a result of which it turned lobster-red.

Viktor, in similar need, did the same.

Sonya came out, looked on in amazement at the two grown-up uncles braving the cold, then retreated into the dacha.

Until nine she watched TV, while Sergey and Viktor played cards. Then they broke off and got the bonfire ready for the New Year kebabs.

"What," asked Sonya, coming out for another look, "have a penguin and the telly got in common?"

Sergey and Viktor exchanged glances.

"Both sleep standing?" Viktor suggested.

"Both black and white," she said, closing the veranda door behind her.

As the fire blazed, Sergey threaded the pieces of meat onto skewers. Viktor stood and watched.

"Do we eat them this year, or next?" he asked jokingly.

"Start them this year, and finish them next," said Sergey. "We've got two kilos of meat!"

When all was prepared, they sat and watched the old favourite *Diamond Arm* on TV. Sonya dropped off before the end, and the friends decided not to wake her until New Year. They moved the kitchen table to the veranda, also the hotplate, and while it warmed the air, spread an old cloth and laid the table. They made a centre piece of the two bottles of champagne and a two-litre bottle of Pepsi, opened the tinned fish, and sliced the cheese and sausage, giving the table a genuinely festive look.

"And one for Misha," declared Sergey, carrying in the low magazine table.

He put it beside their table, and fetched a large dish.

"Poor Misha," he sighed. "Never known a hot meal, or strong drink. Perhaps we should pour him a glass, for the hell of it."

Viktor objected vehemently.

"Sorry, I wasn't serious. What's the time?"

"Nearly eleven."

"In Moscow they'll be clinking glasses already. We can take our seats," said Sergey. "Do we wake Sonya? Or limber up first?"

"Limber up first," said Viktor fetching the already opened bottle of cherry brandy from the kitchen.

Limbering-up completed, Viktor woke Sonya, who at once asked for the TV to be switched on. The voice of the announcer, though unintelligible out on the veranda, seemed, in a strange way, to brighten the proceedings.

"Why hasn't *he* got anything?" she asked, looking at Misha standing beside them.

Dipping into his shopping bag, Viktor brought out a bulging, brightly coloured paper carrier.

"This is his New Year present really," he said, feeling inside, "but we'll take it that it's already New Year in the Antarctic!"

What then emerged was a trade pack, which had to be slit open with a knife, after which Viktor emptied the contents into a large dish on the occasional table.

For a moment all stood in silence, staring – as well they might – at a small octopus, a starfish, king prawns, a lobster and other denizens of the deep now in process of defrosting. Misha, coming to the table to see what his present was, seemed equally amazed.

"You've been lashing out!" said Sergey under his breath. "More than I've ever eaten the like of !"

"Not me, her father – it's from him," whispered Viktor, turning to see if Sonya was listening.

She wasn't. She was leaning forward, pointing at the starfish.

"That's a star," she told Misha, then, pointing to the lobster, "I don't know what that is."

They sat down at the table. The penguin started on the king

prawns without waiting for any special signal. As the television chimes rang out in the living room, Sergey seized a bottle, unwired the cork and gave the bottle a shake. The cork shot out with a pop, and champagne flowed into the cut-glass tumblers. Viktor poured Sonya's Pepsi.

Coloured rockets crackled into the sky from other dacha plots and descended, bathing the winter scene now in green light, now in red. Mingled with the noise of rockets was the sound of actual shots.

"Tokarev semi-automatic," Sergey observed knowledgeably.

The New Year had arrived. The bonfire blazed, lighting up tree and decorations. Rockets shot up from various points around. And in the glassed-in veranda celebrations proceeded apace, with Sergey and Viktor doing justice to the champagne, and Sonya – the Pepsi. Misha, temporarily forgotten, was still standing at his little table. Having finished the prawns, he was sizing up the small octopus.

Once the bonfire had burnt down, they transferred the embers to an iron brazier over which they laid the first three kebabs.

"But the presents – where are my presents?" asked Sonya, coming back to earth.

Viktor reached again into the shopping bag, and brought out two wrapped presents from Misha-non-penguin, and his own, unwrapped, Barbie doll.

"No, not like that!" said Sonya. "Put them all under the tree!"

Dutifully he carried them out.

"There was one for you, too!" she reminded him.

After laying her presents on the snow under the tree, he went back to the veranda. Feeling in the shopping bag for his own present, he was aghast at its shape and weight. Still holding it in the bag, he stripped the coloured paper off, and came to cold metal. There was no doubt about it. Misha-non-penguin's present was a gun. His hands trembled. Without giving it a look, he rewrapped it and zipped up the bag.

"Well, where is it?" shouted Sonya. "We've got to open them together!"

"Forgot it. Left it at home," he shouted back.

Sonya gestured despairingly and gave him a look such as grown-ups reserve for offending children.

"Really! A great big man like you, and you forget!"

But Viktor had gone to join Sergey, who was squatting by the brazier turning the kebabs.

"Come on, show us your presents, Sonya," Sergey called.

She crawled under the tree and sat on the snow. A tearing of paper followed. Viktor went over and bent down to look.

"What is it?" he asked, calmer now, doing his best to feign curiosity.

"A toy," said Sonya.

"What sort? Show me."

"A speaking clock. Like I've seen. Here, listen."

"*0100 hours precisely*," said a metallic female voice.

"And what this is, I've no idea," she muttered, feeling the second present.

Coming from under the tree, she held it out to Viktor.

"What is it?" she asked.

He took it from her. It was a very fat bundle of dollars, held together by elastic bands.

"What is it?" she repeated.

"Money," Viktor said quietly, staring dumbfounded.

"Money?" asked Sergey, joining them.

Bending to look, he started back, thunderstruck.

"It's all hundreds!" he whispered.

"Can I buy things now?" Sonya asked.

"You can," said Viktor.

"A telly?"

"Yes."

"A little house for Barbie?"

"That, too."

"OK, give it to me," she said, taking the bundle of dollars from Viktor. "I'll put it in the dacha."

She climbed the veranda steps.

Sergey gave Viktor quite a look.

"From her father," Viktor said, answering his unspoken question.

Biting his bottom lip, Sergey went and squatted down by the brazier.

"Shame I never had a kind Daddy like that," he whispered.

Viktor wasn't listening. He had a new load on his mind. Presents from Misha-non-penguin entailed obligations, or so it seemed. He remembered his *you answer for her with your life* . . . Rubbish, he thought. Some sort of New Year insanity. Why do I need a gun? Why does she need all that money?

Sergey touched him on the shoulder. "Listen," he said, "I reckon you've been engaged as tutor . . . And she'll be doing the paying!" He gave a smile. "Our kebabs are ready. We can continue to eat . . ."

Viktor welcomed the diversion. He went up the steps to the veranda. Sergey had already taken in the kebabs.

Viktor looked into the main room to call Sonya, but she was already asleep, one hand resting on the bundle of dollars.

Viktor went out as quietly as he could, shutting doors behind him. He took his place at the veranda table and looked round for the penguin. Misha was standing a little way off.

"Well, how about some vodka with our kebabs?" asked Sergey, opening the bottle.

"Good idea!" Viktor held out his empty glass.

After a kebab each and a fair amount of vodka, they retired to bed, overwhelmed with fatigue.

"*0300 hours precisely,*" said the female speaking clock.

37

At getting on for 11.00 the next morning, Viktor was woken by a tapping at the window.

"Your neighbours are here," called a hoarse but cheerful voice. "Happy New Year!"

Going to the window, Viktor saw two young men with girls standing there. The men's faces seemed familiar. He had seen them by the body of the burglar blown up by the mine. Both looked the worse for wear, the girls – not their best.

The one with the beard banged on the window, holding up a bottle of champagne. "Hi! How about a dekko at the penguin?"

Viktor shook the sleeping Sergey.

"We've got visitors!"

"Visitors?" muttered Sergey, but in two minutes he was wide awake.

Soon all were sitting at the table on the veranda. There was plenty of food left and outside, on the extinguished brazier, were the not yet grilled, now refrozen kebabs from the night before.

Having seen their fill of the penguin, the visitors ate, drank and told jokes. Viktor began to find these festivities wearisome and to look forward to their termination. It was not slow in coming. One of the girls suddenly started wailing drunkenly to the effect that she wanted to go to bed, and the visitors very soon left.

Sergey massaged his temples, looking darkly at Viktor. "Work tomorrow," he said sadly.

This set Viktor thinking. He couldn't go back to town yet, and it was too soon to call the Chief.

"Could I stay on a few days more?" he asked.

"Stay forever!" gestured Sergey. "I'm easy. All the better for me – no idiot'll try breaking in."

That evening, in spite of a thumping headache, Sergey set off for Kiev.

"If you need to, ring – there's a public phone, end of main avenue, by the caretaker's place," he said as he left. "I'll tell Security you're here. But I'd be a bit more careful with that wad of hundreds . . . Hide it away somewhere."

Viktor nodded.

The *Zaporozhets* sprang into life and departed. Silence returned. Except for faint sounds from the living room where Sonya was watching a film on TV.

"Shouldn't I look after that money for you?" asked Viktor, perching beside her on the settee.

"Here," she said, handing him the bundle. "Only don't lose it."

Putting the dollars with the gift gun into the shopping bag, he dropped both into the cellar.

38

The next few days passed quietly and uneventfully, apart from the arrival of the local militia to collect the body of the hapless burglar, when, at the request of the caretaker, Vanya, everyone kept indoors. "Not keen to appear as witnesses, are we?" he had asked, and Viktor agreed that he wasn't.

When the militia had gone, Vanya came around with the all-clear.

"It's OK," he said.

"Won't the owner of the dacha be in trouble?" Viktor enquired.

Grandpa Vanya grinned.

"The Colonel? He's just been. Reckoned they'd put the mine there for him, not the thief. *Obvious, he said, wasn't it? Lots of that sort of thing about nowadays.*"

Sonya spent most of her time in front of the TV, and only when something really boring was on did she go outside or potter with the penguin on the veranda.

Viktor found idleness difficult to bear. He wanted to do something, *anything*, however useless. But at the dacha there was nothing to do, and he was miserable, first joining Sonya in front of the TV for a bit, then sitting in the kitchen, to where he had moved back the table and hotplate from the veranda.

Unable, finally, to endure it any more, and telling Sonya not to go out, he went and rang the Chief from the public phone.

It was the secretary who answered.

"Can I speak to Igor Lvovich?"

"I'll take it, Tanya," intervened the familiar voice. "Yes?"

"It's me, Viktor. Can I come back yet?"

"Didn't know you'd gone away," said the Chief, feigning surprise. "Of course. Everything's fine. Come and see me as soon as you can. Got something to show you."

Viktor then rang Sergey asking him to pick them up as soon as possible.

Walking back to the dacha, he was in a happier frame of mind. At last New Year had an aura of holiday about it, albeit of a holiday now past. Again, the crunch of snow, but now it was a cheerful sound. Looking about him, he took in what so far he had not noticed: the sculptural beauty of winter trees, of bullfinches wandering over snow covered with tracks of cat, or dog. And from forgotten depths surfaced a memory of natural history lessons at which, long, long ago, they had learnt to identify animal prints; and of text-book illustrations – *Tracks of the hare . . . Hopping . . . Bounding . . .* And out of the past, the voice of his first lady teacher: "The hare, when fleeing pursuit, *bounds!*"

39

Leaving the shopping bag with gun and bundle of dollars on top of the wardrobe, and Sonya at home with Misha, Viktor set off for the editorial office.

Smiling smugly, the Chief sat him in an armchair, produced coffee, asked about the New Year festivities, blatantly putting off any mention of business. When, after coffee, a pause ensued which it would clearly have been foolish to fill with idle conversation, he produced a large envelope from his desk drawer.

Keeping his eyes fixed on Viktor, he drew out several photographs and passed them over.

"Take a look. You may know them."

The photos showed two well-dressed corpses. Young men of 25 or so lying on the floor of someone's flat, tidily and obediently supine – no outflung arms, splayed legs or faces distorted by fear or agony. Their faces were calm, indifferent.

"Don't recognize them?"

"No," said Viktor.

"You were their target . . . Here's a memento!" He passed over two more photos.

Viktor saw himself at the little table in the café beneath the Kharkov Opera House; and in the street, also in Kharkov.

"Modest lads," said the Chief, "only one silencer between them . . . Anyway, they didn't get to you. But the negatives are still somewhere in Kharkov . . . I don't think they'll send anyone else, but watch it."

Finally, he handed Viktor a batch of fresh *obelisk* material.

"So, quietly back to work," he said, patting Viktor on the shoulder and seeing him out.

40

In January winter was lazy to the extent of making do with December's snow which, thanks to continuing frost, still blanketed the earth. Shop windows still had their New Year decorations, but the festive spirit had waned, leaving folk alone with the old routine and the future. Viktor was processing his next batch of files. He now received all documents direct from the Chief, Fyodor having retired before the New Year break.

The *obelisk* index was growing steadily. These latest files were on directors of major factories and chairmen of joint-stock companies. Almost all were charged with the theft of funds and their transfer to Western banks. Some were dealing in banned raw materials, others contriving to barter off plant abroad. Facts were legion, but mercifully not all were underlined in the Chief's red pencil. Viktor's task was not easy. He either ran short of philosophy, or lacked inspiration, as each *obelisk* now involved tense hours at the typewriter. And though, in the end, he was pleased with the result, fatigue weighed heavily upon him, leaving little energy to spare for Sonya or the penguin. So it was as well that he had, at Sonya's insistence, bought a colour television on their return from the dacha. And now they came together in front of it, but always with Sonya in charge of the remote control.

"It's my telly!" she said, which Viktor, having in fact bought it with her money, had to concede.

Misha also took an interest in the television, sometimes going right up to the screen and blocking Viktor and Sonya's view. Sonya would then gently lead him off to the bedroom, where he liked to stand in front of the mirror studying his reflection. Viktor was surprised how easily she managed him. Although that was not surprising perhaps, seeing that she spent far more time with him than he did. Several times she even took him for a walk on the waste area by the dovecotes.

One evening the doorbell rang, and seeing a complete stranger through the spyhole, he was filled with alarm. He at once thought back to the photos of the two dead young men who had been after him. Sighing audibly, the stranger, a man of about 40, gave the button another press, jangling the bell right above where Viktor stood with bated breath.

Behind him the living-room door creaked and Sonya called: "Do go to the door. Someone's ringing!"

"Open up. Nothing to be afraid of," came a voice from the other side of the door.

"Who do you want?"

"You! Who else! What are you afraid of? I've come about Misha."

Viktor reached for the lock, wondering which Misha, and finally opened the door.

A thin, unshaven, sharp-nosed man in a Chinese down jacket and a black knitted hat came in. From his pocket, he pulled out a sheet of paper folded in two or three, and passed it to Viktor.

"My calling card," he said with a grin.

An icy shiver ran down Viktor's spine as he unfolded it and held it up to read. It was his *obelisk* on Misha-non-penguin's friend-cum-enemy, Sergey Chekalin.

"Know me now?" asked the visitor coldly.

"Sergey Chekalin," said Viktor, and seeing Sonya still standing in the open door, told her sternly to go back in, before turning again to his visitor.

"Could we sit down somewhere? We need to talk."

Viktor took him into the kitchen, where he sat straight down in Viktor's chair, leaving him to sit opposite.

"Got some bad news," said the visitor. "Misha, I'm sorry to say, is dead. And I've come for his daughter. There's no longer any sense in keeping her hidden. OK?"

Very slowly, bit by bit, what had been said got through to Viktor. But the two basic facts: that Misha was dead and that this

97

man had come for Sonya, somehow refused to connect. He put his hand to his forehead, as if at a sudden stab of pain, and it was as cold as ice.

"How did he die?" Viktor asked suddenly, looking down at the table top, his expression one of dismay.

"How?" Sergey responded. "As they all do, tragically."

"And why does she have to go with you?" Viktor asked after a short pause to collect his thoughts.

"I was his friend. It's my duty to look after her."

Viktor shook his head. The visitor stared, astonished.

"No," said Viktor, his voice suddenly firmer. "Misha wanted *me* to look after her."

"Listen," said his visitor wearily, "with all due respect to your protection, you've got it wrong. And can you prove he wanted you to?"

"I have a note from him," Viktor said calmly. "I'll show you."

"Do that."

Viktor went into the living room and searched through a sheaf of papers on the window ledge for Misha's note promising to be back when the dust settled. As he turned to where Sonya and the penguin were absorbed watching figure skating on the TV, he heard the front door bang. He went and poked his head into the kitchen. His visitor had beaten an unceremonious retreat, leaving his obituary on the kitchen table.

A few minutes later an engine started up. Viktor looked out, and in the light of a street lamp, saw a long car just like Misha-non-penguin's moving off.

"What did that man come for?" Sonya asked, looking into the kitchen.

"For you," he said under his breath, without turning to her.

"What did he come for?" she repeated, not having heard.

"Just for a talk."

She went back to the TV, and Viktor sat down at the kitchen table to think – about his life, and Sonya's part in it. An inconspicuous one, it might seem, but one that still bound him to look after her and think about her. Except that *looking after* amounted to no more than food and the odd conversation. Sonya's presence in his life was much like that of Misha the penguin in his flat. Still, when someone had turned up to take her away, alarm had given rise to sudden determination. Again there had been talk of *protection*, of *security*, of which he knew nothing. His life was split in two halves, one known, one unknown. And what was in the other half? What did it consist of? He bit his lip. Riddles were the last thing he wanted to contend with. The Chief's red pencil had trained him in the use of basic facts as starting points for any text or idea. That evening he was hard put to it to determine which of the ideas dancing around inside his head would, when committed to paper, merit red pencil.

41

It was strange, but in a couple of days Viktor had forgotten Sergey Chekalin's visit, being, after a polite telephonic hastener from the Chief, completely absorbed in his work. In brief breaks between *obelisks* he drank tea and thought that he ought to devote more attention to Sonya, take her to the puppet theatre and that sort of thing. But all that would have to be deferred pending more free time. One way he did manage to make the little girl happy was with the ice-cream and other sweets he now purchased in large quantities. Shopping excursions provided his only opportunities for a breath of fresh, frosty air. The more frequently he sallied forth, the happier Sonya and Misha were. Sonya's happiness, unlike Misha's, took vocal expression. More often than not she called him Uncle Vik, and that pleased him. But the main thing was that she didn't object to spending most of her time in the flat. And in the evening, when they sat in front of the TV watching the latest episode of a Mexican serial, Viktor had a calm, comfortable feeling, while giving no thought to what he was watching. He was enjoying this winter. Anything bad was quickly forgotten over work, or in front of the TV.

"Uncle Vik," began Sonya, pointing at the screen, "why does Alejandra have a nanny?"

"I expect she's got rich parents."

"Are you rich?"

Viktor shrugged. "Not very . . ."

"Am I?"

He turned and looked at her.

"Me, am I rich?" she asked again.

"Yes," he nodded. "Richer than me."

It was a conversation he recalled the next day during one of his tea breaks. How much a nanny cost he had no idea, but the notion of engaging one for Sonya came that day as a revelation.

That evening his district militiaman friend looked in with a bottle of red wine. They sat in the kitchen. Wet snow was falling and flakes were sticking to the window pane.

Sergey was a bit on edge.

"Do you know, I've been offered a district militia job in Moscow. Ten times what I'm paid here . . . Free flat."

Viktor shrugged. "But you know what it's like there," he said. "Shooting, explosions . . ."

"Got that here, too," said Sergey. "But it's not Special Task I'm joining . . . I'll be what I am now . . . I don't know – maybe I'll go for a year, earn a bit of money."

"Up to you."

"Yes." Sergey sighed. "How about your troubles? Over and done with?"

"Looks like it."

"Let's hope so."

"Don't happen to know of some normal young woman, do you?" Viktor enquired earnestly. "I'm looking for a nanny for Sonya . . . Reliable and not too expensive?"

Sergey thought. "I've got a niece. Twenty. Unemployed. Like me to ask?"

Viktor nodded.

"How much a month would you offer?"

"$50?"

"Right," said Sergey.

42

Next day, out of the blue, the old penguinologist phoned.

"It's me, Pidpaly," he said weakly. "That you, Viktor?"

"Yes."

"Could you come? I'm feeling ill."

Putting his work aside, Viktor set off for Svyatoshino.

The old man was pale. His hands were shaking. The skin

below his sunken eyes was yellow.

"Come in," he said, visibly cheered.

The room was warm and stuffy.

"What's the matter?"

"I don't know . . . Stomach pains. Three days I haven't slept," the old man complained, sitting down at the table.

"Have you called a doctor?"

Pidpaly waved an arm dismissively. "What for? What am I to them? No money to be got out of me."

Viktor went to the phone and called an ambulance.

"No point!" Another dismissive wave. "They'll come, and go away. I know them."

"Sit where you are," Viktor ordered. "I'll make tea."

The kitchen table was a heap of dirty crockery and leftovers. The cups had soggy cigarette ends in them. He washed out two of the cups in the sink and put the kettle on.

Time passed. The tea was ready and they sat at the table in silence and a state of expectancy. The ghost of an ironic smile played over the old man's features. From time to time he shot Viktor a glance.

"I told you, I *did once* come in for the better things of this life," he said didactically, his voice hoarse and feeble.

Viktor said nothing.

At last, the doorbell rang. A paramedic and an orderly entered.

"Who's the patient?" asked the paramedic, teasing burnt tobacco from a just-extinguished cigarette with the fingers of his right hand.

Viktor nodded at the old man. "He is."

"What's the trouble?" The paramedic scanned Pidpaly's face.

"My stomach . . . Here."

"Give him Papaverine?" queried the paramedic turning to the orderly, who was gazing sourly around at the walls.

"No need. Won't do any good," said Pidpaly. "I've had some."

"Well, that's all we've got," said the paramedic helplessly. "So we'll be on our way." Beckoning to the orderly, he turned to go.

"Hang on!" said Viktor.

The paramedic looked back.

"What?"

"Could you get him to a hospital?"

"We could, but who'd take him in?" he asked, heaving an almost genuine sigh.

Viktor produced $50.

"Isn't there somewhere?" he asked.

The paramedic dithered, looked again at the old man, as if gaugeing his value.

"The October might," he shrugged, sidling up, awkwardly taking the proffered note and thrusting it into the pocket of his grubby smock.

Leaning over the table and locating a pencil and piece of paper, Viktor jotted down his telephone number.

"Ring and let me know how he is and where he is," he said, handing it over.

The paramedic nodded.

"Come on then," he flung at the old man.

Pidpaly flapped around, went unsteadily to the kitchen, and came back jingling something in his shaky hand.

"Have these keys, Vik," he said, "and lock up when you go."

The paramedic and the orderly waited patiently while the old man dressed, then led him away, more like a prisoner than a patient.

Alone in the strange flat, Viktor sat for a while at the table, breathing stuffy, dusty air overlaid with an irritant odour of humid warmth. He didn't feel right. Eventually he got to his feet, but was reluctant to go. It was a home in ruins, this flat, and it moved him to genuine pity. The very walls bore the stamp of their owner's helplessness, as did everything within them, together with an air of total isolation.

He washed up and tidied things a bit before leaving. Let Pidpaly at least come back to comparative comfort for a day or two, he thought, locking up behind him.

That evening the nameless paramedic phoned.

"Not long for this world, that old man – it's cancer," he said.

"Where is he?"

"October Hospital, Oncology, Ward 5."

"Thanks." Viktor replaced the receiver.

Saddened, he looked round at Sonya.

"Are we going to the waste area today?" she asked, catching his eye.

"Supper first," he said, making for the kitchen.

43

A couple of days later, the Chief's courier arrived with a fresh batch of files. Glancing over them, Viktor saw he was now dealing with senior ranks of the military. About 20 were due for *obelisks*, all featuring nostalgia for the past seamlessly combined with arms dealing. Beyond that, it was every man for himself – even to the extent of ferrying illegal emigrants over the Ukrainian–Polish frontier in military helicopters, and the permanent renting out of transport aircraft. The further he read, the grimmer it got. But this bunch had something about them that marked them out from previous notables. Putting the papers aside, he thought about it, looking out at on-going winter. He gathered up the papers again. They had all been good husbands and fathers, these generals, colonels and majors, morally sound to a man.

Another read through, and he was in the mood for work. He put the kettle on and fetched out the typewriter from under the table.

He worked away for two hours, until distracted by the phone. It was district militiaman Sergey.

"I've had a word with my niece," he said, "and she's happy to come. I'll bring her along in half an hour, if that's all right."

"Good."

The darkness of a winter evening was descending early over the city. Putting work aside, Viktor went and sat in the living room. Sonya was playing with her Barbie doll.

"Where's Misha?" he asked.

"In there."

"Sonya, we've got an auntie coming," he said, "a young auntie who's going to be your nanny."

Feeling he had put it clumsily, he paused.

"Will she play with me, Uncle Vik?" Sonya asked.

"Of course."

"What's she called?"

"I don't know," he admitted. "She's a niece of Uncle Sergey, whose dacha we went to for New Year."

The doorbell rang. Getting to his feet, Viktor looked at his watch. A bit early, he thought, for Sergey. But Sergey it was.

"This is Nina," said Sergey, as they removed their jackets in the corridor.

Viktor shook hands, took Nina's jacket, and hung it on a peg.

"This is Sonya," he told Nina as they gathered in the living room.

Nina gave her a smile.

"And this," he told Sonya, "is Nina."

Again he was tongue-tied by the awkwardness of the situation, half expecting the little girl and the young lady to talk away, making him superfluous. Instead, they looked at one another and said nothing. Viktor, meanwhile, took in Nina: small, round-faced, short chestnut hair, looking about 17, in close-fitting jeans emphasizing a certain plumpness, and a blue sweater gently outlining small breasts. There was something of the teenager about her – the smile, perhaps, though that was visibly restrained. The reason, he soon saw, being to hide yellow-stained teeth. Probably a smoker, he thought.

"I can begin tomorrow," she said suddenly.

"And what shall we do?" Sonya asked.

Nina smiled her half-smile. "What do you want to do?"

"Go tobogganing."

"Have you got a toboggan?"

"Have I?" asked Sonya with a wide-eyed, skittish glance at Viktor.

"No," he confessed.

"Don't worry, I'll bring one," Nina said quickly, as if to forestall anything Viktor might say. "Transport's good from Podol where I live."

Viktor nodded.

It was agreed that Nina would come at ten and take care of Sonya until five.

Having seen Sergey and his niece out, Viktor sighed with twofold relief. To his delight, the business side of their conversation had proved less than mercenary, and more to the point, Sonya now had a nanny. He felt more comfortable, more relaxed for the future.

"Well, what do you think?" he asked, returning to the living room.

"She's all right." Sonya said cheerfully. "We'll see what Misha thinks of her!"

44

For Viktor, the arrival of Nina was a kind of liberation. Not because he had previously given a lot of time to Sonya – he was giving just as much now – breakfast, supper, the same evening television sessions together. But he was still left with the feeling of having considerably more time, not necessarily free time, but just time – simply by virtue of reproaching himself less, thinking less often of Sonya and no longer accusing himself of not doing anything with her. Now Nina came for her in the morning, and they set off together he knew not where, and in the evening a weary Sonya would boast, *We walked around Hydropark* or *We've been to Pushcha-Voditsa!*

Viktor was happy. Work was making quiet progress. Winter was relenting. Misha was again roaming the flat at night, and once scared Sonya into screaming. She had been sleeping with her arm hanging over the side of the settee, when Misha bumped, then nestled against it.

She had probably been dreaming, and the sudden physical warmth of Misha had produced a nightmare effect.

Having finished the military, Viktor decided not to ring the Chief for further files, but take a day off. It was sunny, and a pre-spring thaw was in progress.

Sonya and Nina had gone for a walk again. Misha, after a solid breakfast, had returned to the living room, and was standing by the balcony door, where the cold was to his liking.

Viktor decided to pay old Pidpaly a visit.

The thaw had made the pavements treacherous, and on his way to the October Hospital he had several falls, the last of them on the steps of Oncology.

Ward 5, which he located unaided, was huge, like a school gymnasium. To some extent, and probably by reason of the strict alternation of beds and bedside tables, it was like a barracks. Not a nurse was to be seen. A sour medicinal odour pervaded the place. Some beds were screened off.

After a good look round he spotted Pidpaly, lying staring at the ceiling, on a bed by a window. His head seemed to have shrunk.

Picking up a heavy stool inside the door, he went and sat by the penguinologist's bed, but went unnoticed.

"Hello," said Viktor.

Pidpaly turned, and his thin pale lips extended into a smile. "Greetings."

"How are we? Are you getting treatment?"

A smile was the old man's response.

"I didn't bring anything," Viktor said guiltily, noticing two oranges on a neighbouring bedside table. "Somehow I didn't think."

"No matter . . . the good thing is you've come." The old man extricated an arm from under the blanket of grey greatcoat material, raised it to his face and fingered the stubble on his flabby cheeks. "The barber comes once a week, on Friday. Gets paid only for two hours, so he'll never get to me."

"And you want your hair cut?" Seeing how little hair he had, Viktor was surprised.

"A shave is what I want," said the old man again, fingering his stubble. "My previous neighbour," he nodded at the bed on the right, "gave me his shaving kit. The whole works. Brush and all. But I can't shave myself . . ."

"Like me to?" ventured Viktor.

"If you would."

Taking the razor, brush and squat plastic beaker, also part of the kit, from Pidpaly's bedside table, Viktor got to his feet.

"I'll just fetch some water."

He walked the whole length of the corridor twice in search of a nurse or doctor, without finding either. He did find a toilet, but the water from the tap was cold. In the end he enquired of a patient, who sent him to the kitchen, one floor down. There an old woman in a blue smock looked out a half-litre jar, and filled it with hot water from a boiler for him.

The actual shave took the best part of an hour, the razor being old and the blade blunt. He could see the cuts left on the old man's cheeks, but no blood came. When at last he had finished, he collected Eau de Cologne from others in the ward, and pouring a little into his palm, rubbed it on the old man's cheeks. Pidpaly groaned.

"Sorry," Viktor said mechanically.

"No matter," said the old man hoarsely. "Means you're still alive if it hurts."

"What does the doctor say?"

"Give my flat over to him and he'll give me another three months." Again he smiled. "But what's three months to me? I've no unfinished business."

Viktor's right hand balled itself into a fist.

"Do they give you no medicines?" he asked.

"There aren't any. Those who bring them, get given them. For the others, it's bed and rest."

Viktor said nothing, waiting for his fury to abate.

"And what did he offer for your flat?" he asked when calmer. "Medicines?"

"Some sort of American injections . . ." The old man put a hand to his shaven cheek. "Look, there's something I want to ask you . . ." He edged towards Viktor, turning with an effort onto his side. "Bend down closer."

Viktor bent down closer.

"You've got the flat keys?" he whispered.

"Yes," Viktor whispered back.

"Listen. Don't let me down. When I die, set fire to my flat," whispered the old man. "I beg you! Don't want anyone sitting in my chair, rummaging in my papers, rubbish-binning the lot. Understand? It's my things . . . What I've lived with, and don't want to leave here . . . Understand?"

Viktor nodded.

"Promise you will when I'm dead," he said, gazing questioningly, beseechingly into Viktor's eyes.

"I promise," Viktor whispered.

"That's good." Again the bloodless lips formed a smile. "I told you, I *did once* come in for the better things of this life, didn't I?"

With a heavy sigh he turned onto his back again.

"So off with you," he said hoarsely. "Thanks for the shave. Otherwise, it's lie unshaven, like a corpse!" He pointed to the nearest screen.

"Is that one?" Viktor whispered uneasily.

"Screen today, morgue tomorrow!" whispered Pidpaly. "Off you go."

Viktor got to his feet, stood for a moment looking down at Pidpaly. But Pidpaly was gazing at the ceiling, thin lips moving as if shaping words audible to no one but himself.

45

The next day began as usual. The sun shone in at the window, and Viktor and Sonya sat at a breakfast of fried eggs and tea in the kitchen. Misha, moody since daybreak, refused, however much cajoled, to come and join them.

Sonya kept casting eager looks at the alarm clock on the window ledge, as if willing the minute hand forward.

At 9.40 the doorbell rang and she darted out, almost knocking her stool over.

Nina had arrived. A happy exchange of greetings ensued, after which Nina, still in her coat, looked in to say hello.

"Where are you off to today?" Viktor asked.

"Syrets. Walk in the woods, then to Podol and to my place for lunch."

She gave a dutiful nod and a teeth-concealing half-smile.

"So where's your little jacket?" he heard her asking Sonya in the corridor. "And now your little boots."

Five minutes later she looked in again.

"Just off," she said, with another half-smile.

The door banged. Silence descended, except for a faint stirring in the living room. The door creaked open, and Misha peeped out. Apparently satisfied that the corridor was empty, he advanced to the kitchen door and pushed it open. He contemplated his master from the doorway, then came over and snuggled up against his knee. Viktor stroked him.

After several minutes of this, Misha went to his bowl, and stood looking back. Viktor took two small plaice out of the freezer, cut them up and gave them to him. He then returned to his seat, having topped up his cup of tea.

The relative silence – apart from the sound of Misha's breakfasting – took Viktor back to when there had been just the two of them living there in peace and quiet, without any sense of strong attachment, but with a feeling of interdependence creating a kind of blood tie between them – as if, in the absence of love, there was concern. After all, even relatives didn't have to be loved – taken care of, worried about, yes, but feelings and emotions were of secondary importance in that, and not, so long as all was well with them, obligatory . . .

Making short work of his breakfast, Misha returned to his master who, struck by this unusually affectionate behaviour, stroked him, at which he pressed more firmly against his knee. "Not feeling ill, are we?" he asked gently, looking him over.

We seem to have been neglecting you, he thought. First it was the TV with Sonya, now it's Nina. I'm sorry. And there was I thinking you and Sonya were playing as you used to. I'm sorry . . . Viktor sat on at the kitchen table for a good 20 minutes, not wanting to disturb Misha, considering the recent past and

112

thinking about the future. Life, despite the short-lived dangers he had sat out at the dacha over New Year, seemed on an even course. All was well, or appeared so. To every time, its own *normality*. The once terrible was now commonplace, meaning that people accepted it as the norm and went on living, instead of getting needlessly agitated. For them, as for Viktor, the main thing, after all, was still *to live*, come what might.

The thaw continued.

At about two the doorbell rang. Expecting it to be Nina and Sonya, he went to the door, but it was Igor Lvovich who marched in, banging the door behind him, took off his coat, and went through to the kitchen without removing his footwear.

Pale, baggy-eyed, the Chief was clearly not himself.

"Make some coffee," he said, plumping himself down in Viktor's place.

Seeing to coffee-maker and coffee, Viktor looked back at the Chief. He appeared to be trembling, and for just an instant Viktor felt similarly affected. He lit the burner, poured coffee and water into the coffee-maker, and put it on the flame.

"So what!" the Chief was muttering abstractedly. "So what!"

"Has something happened?"

"It has," said Igor Lvovich, looking away. "Just wait . . . Till I warm up . . ."

Again silence. Viktor stood watching the coffee. As the foam rose, he took the coffee-maker off the heat, fetched cups and poured.

Hands clasped round the cup, the Chief looked across at him. "Thanks," he said.

Viktor sat down at the table with him.

"Look," the Chief began suddenly, "it's best I tell you nothing.

113

What's it to you? Remember how *you* had to lie low for a day or two?"

Viktor nodded.

"Well," he smiled wrily, "now it's *my* turn. Just for a day or two. Till the boys clear the way. Then back to the grind."

"I've done all the military," said Viktor. "They're there, on the window ledge."

In no mood for *obelisks*, the Chief dismissed them with a wave.

He drank his coffee, lit a cigarette, and looking in vain for an ashtray, used the table instead, and for some minutes sat lost in thought.

"It's hard, you know, finding you've been put on the spot by your own." He sighed. "Very hard . . . Busy just now?"

"No."

"Well then," said the Chief, looking earnestly at him, "you can go to my office for me – I'll ring my secretary to let you in – and bring back the brown briefcase from the safe. I'll give you the key. If you find you're being followed, ditch the key, and wander round till dark."

Viktor suddenly felt afraid. Gulping his coffee, he looked up and into a steady gaze dismissive of any thoughts or qualms.

"When?" he asked, like a doomed man.

"Now."

The Chief handed over a key from his wallet.

"But wait till I've rung through," he said, as Viktor rose from the table.

The Chief went to the living room.

"Off you go," he said, returning.

Thaw or no thaw, it was freezing, of which none was more aware than Viktor, walking slowly to the trolleybus stop, no longer afraid, but mind and whole body numb with cold.

When, an hour later, he entered the newspaper building, he had to show his Press card to three lots of Special Task Militia before finally arriving at the Editor-in-Chief's reception. The pale secretary nodded recognition, and without a word, unlocked the Chief's sanctum. Having closed the door behind him, Viktor found himself trembling all over, and remembering he hadn't once checked to see if he was being followed, felt suddenly afraid.

To calm himself, he went over to the desk and sat in the Chief's chair. The safe was to his left, on a low table. He got out the key. After a moment or so's hesitation, he opened the safe. The brown briefcase was on the lower shelf. He placed it on the desk before him. Once again trembling precluded thought. He had no inclination to get to his feet and leave the office, as if he were aware of danger lurking beyond its walls. He had another look in the safe, to spin out time. On the upper shelf lay a folder with several typed sheets on top. Without thinking, he reached for the topmost sheet, and recognized it at once as his *obelisk* for the Director of Ferro-Concrete Reinforcements. In the top left-hand corner someone had written

Approved.
For 14.02.99

with a bold, sweeping signature.

His growing astonishment proved a release from fear and trembling. *Today was only February the third!* A glance at the other sheets confirmed that they, too, were recent *obelisks*, each *approved* for some date ahead. Returning to the safe, he took out the folder and untied the ribbons. More *obelisks*, the more or less recent on top, all of them *approved* – one for that very day, the

115

third, and with the same bold, sweeping signature. He extracted some from the middle of the pile. The first of these, as well as *approved* for a date now past had

Processed

written in a different hand.

With his head in a whirl, Viktor sat staring at the brown briefcase, the *obelisks*, the open safe, and suddenly there was a nasty bitter taste in his mouth. He picked up one of the papers lying on the desk. It was a letter to the printers, word-processed except for the signature, and this he studied closely. It wasn't the Chief who had written *approved* on the *obelisks*. His signature, unlike the bold, sweeping one, was straightforward and legible. But something about it still seemed familiar, and looking back at the old obituary from the middle of the pile, he saw that *Processed* had been written in the same unsteady, shivering-with-cold characters.

The phone on the desk rang, and he jumped guiltily. He looked at it, expecting it to stop, but it didn't. And again he was gripped by fear. He looked about him, as if to check whether he was being watched, and suddenly spotted the lens of a video camera mounted on a bracket directly above the door and pointing down at him.

Slipping the *obelisks* back in the folder, he returned it to the safe with the others, and locking the safe, stole a last look at the video camera. The phone had stopped ringing, but the renewed silence was no less intimidating. Fearful of disturbing it, he got gingerly to his feet, picked up the briefcase, and left.

The secretary turned from her computer and the graphic escape-from-pursuit game frozen on its screen. She looked tense.

"Finished already?" she asked.

With difficulty he managed a *Thank you* and a *Goodbye*.

46

Oblivious to the city, looking neither to left nor right, he made for home, tightly gripping the handle of the briefcase. His feet knew the way.

Not until he was actually at the door of his flat did it register that, sitting on a bench down at the entrance, there had been a young man in training suit and woolly ski hat watching him closely. Having got the door open, he stopped, listened, and hearing no sound from the entrance below, went on in, carefully shutting it behind him.

"Well?" said the Chief coming out into the corridor to meet him.

Seeing the briefcase, he smiled and bore it off to the kitchen.

By the time Viktor had removed his boots and jacket, Igor Lvovich had the contents of his briefcase – green trident-embossed diplomatic passport, credit cards, notebook and receipts – spread out on the table.

"Down at the entrance," said Viktor, "there's a young chap sitting –"

"I know. One of ours," confirmed the Chief without looking up. "Got anything to eat? I'm peckish."

The Chief was his old self again, calm, confident, steady as a rock, intrepid.

Opening the fridge, Viktor got out polonies, butter and mustard, and proceeded to the stove, now with his back to the Chief, but with the acrid taste of the Chief's tobacco in his mouth.

As he lit the gas, he heard the Chief get up and go through to the living room, and while the water boiled, could just hear him talking to someone on the phone, but had no inclination to turn and listen. His instinct was to keep his back turned on all that was happening, and let it happen unseen, away from him and his life.

Again the door creaked, footsteps sounded, a stool scraped. The Chief was back at the table.

The polonies were already in boiling water.

"Got any dollars handy?" asked the Chief.

"Some," said Viktor without turning.

"You can lend me $800."

After that they ate in silence, Viktor kept an an eye on the old alarm clock on the window ledge. It was getting on for four. Nina would soon be bringing Sonya. And what then? What did the Chief have in mind? To lie low here? For how long? And where would it all end?

Viktor dipped his little circles of sliced polony in the mustard and munched mechanically. Something was missing, he felt suddenly, then saw that it was bread. But across the table the Chief was eating away just as happily without. Instead of dipping each little fork-impaled circle in mustard like Viktor, he doused it in melted butter before conveying it to his mouth.

"Tea," ordered the Chief, pushing away his empty plate.

Viktor made tea. Again they sat opposite each other in silence. The Chief was busy with his own thoughts, and watching him, Viktor thought of the notes adorning his *obelisks*. He would have liked to know who and what lay behind those *approveds*, but was more than certain that the Chief wouldn't say, but would put him off with a *What's that to you?* and that would be that.

He sighed, and the Chief, his train of thought broken, shot him a look.

"Another job for you," he said. "Collect my air ticket, Victory

Square, Window 12, taking the $800 with you. You'll get them back. Flight booking 503."

It was getting dark. Viktor didn't feel like going out again, but knew that he had to, whether he liked it or not.

"All right," he said, but tardily enough to earn a look of surprise, which was replaced by a weary smile.

Viktor put on his jacket and boots. As he left the block, he noted, out of the corner of his eye, the continuing presence of the sportsman in the knitted ski hat.

Apart from a lone Azerbaijani dolefully studying a flight timetable, the airline booking offices were deserted.

At Window 12 was a woman of about 40, with blue-rinsed hair piled high.

"Booking 503," he said.

"Passport," she responded, without looking up, tapping the booking into her computer.

Not having the Chief's passport, Viktor was sunk.

"Ah!" breathed the window lady suddenly. "*No passport required. It's all here. $750 at exchange rate or $800 cash*," she said, pointing to the pay desk, still without looking up.

Viktor handed over eight $100 bills. They were counted by a young lady in a blue uniform who put them through a forgery detector, turned and shouted, "Cash received, Vera."

Window 12 gave him the ticket. For *Kiev–Larnaca–Rome*. He folded it and placed it in an inner pocket of his jacket.

It was about six when he reached the flat. Nina and Sonya were still not back. The Chief was still sitting in the kitchen, having earlier brewed coffee which he was now calmly drinking.

He studied the ticket carefully before concealing it in his wallet.

"Nobody been?" Viktor asked.

119

"Who are you expecting?"

"Sonya's nanny should be bringing her."

"No, no one's been," said the Chief thoughtfully. "But I'd advise getting her to take the little girl to her place for the night." To add weight to his words, he nodded in the manner of one imparting wisdom.

Nina brought Sonya at 6.30, full of apologies for being so late.

"I hope you weren't worried," she said, while still in the corridor. "I *am* sorry. We got delayed at the station. Seeing Sergey off."

"I wasn't worried," said Viktor. "But Nina, could Sonya possibly stay with you for tonight?"

Nina looked at him in surprise. Sonya, who had already taken her boots off but was still wearing her jacket, was looking too, though more in curiosity than surprise.

"Of course," said the puzzled Nina.

"Hold on." Viktor went to the bedroom and returned with $100.

"That's for this week and for your trouble."

"When do you want her back?"

"Tomorrow . . . Late afternoon."

Alone in the corridor, Viktor sighed. Noticing bootmarks and puddles of melted snow on the linoleum, he fetched a rag from the lavatory and mopped them up before returning to the kitchen.

"Sit with me till half past one," the Chief said quietly. "I've a car coming, and as I'm tired, I might fall asleep . . . Got any cards?"

The time passed surprisingly slowly. It had long been dark, and the city was hushed. They played Preference-with-dummy, keeping a note of their stakes. Viktor kept losing. The Chief smiled as he played, glancing occasionally at the alarm clock. At intervals he lit another cigarette, and as the mound of ash on the left of the table grew, he moulded it into a little pyramid.

At 1.30 exactly the car arrived. The Chief looked out of the window, then totted up his winnings.

"$95 you owe me," he grinned. "You'll win it back!"

He got to his feet and put on his coat.

"Have a holiday," he said, preparing to leave. "When the dust settles, I'll return, and we'll continue the good work."

"But, Igor, what is the real point of my work?" Viktor asked, stopping him in his tracks.

The Chief considered him through narrowed eyes.

"Your interest lies in not asking questions," he said quietly. "Think what you like. But bear in mind this: the moment you *are* told what the point of your work is, you're dead. This isn't a film, it's for real. The full story is what you get told only if and when your work, and with it your existence, are no longer required." He smiled a sad smile. "Still, I do, in fact, wish you well. Believe me."

He opened the door, and there was the familiar sportsman. The latter gave a nod and he and the Chief set off down the stairs.

Viktor shut the door. The silence of the flat was unnerving. The tang of tobacco was bitter in his mouth, and he had a sudden urge to spit to rid himself of it.

Back in the kitchen the air was even thicker with tobacco smoke – almost opaque. He opened the window vent. He felt the cold air, but the smoke, illuminated by the bulb, refused to budge, as if the air was still, despite the open vent. Removing his papers from the window ledge, he threw the window open. An icy blast slammed the kitchen door shut. Gradually the haze dispersed. With the cold came fresh air. He was indifferent to the wind, but watched it blow the chief's pyramid of ash across the table, reducing it to tiny specks which it rolled to

121

the edge of the table and over. In the end, no trace of the little pyramid remained.

The door opened and there, attracted by the cold, was Misha. Coming over to his master, he stood gazing up at him.

Viktor gave him a smile. He had another look to make sure the air was clear of smoke. Dazzled suddenly by the kitchen bulb, he switched it off and sat in the dark.

47

Viktor woke at about eleven feeling cold. Jumping out of bed, he ran to the kitchen, closed the window and vent, and went straight back to the bedroom. For a while he lay in bed in his clothes to warm himself, then got up again.

After a hot bath and some strong coffee he felt better, and gradually warmth returned to the flat. He remembered the events of the day before – what had been written on his obituaries in the safe, the airline booking office, cards until 1.30 in the morning. It all seemed to have happened not the day before, but long ago, in the distant past. Then, as he caught a sudden whiff of tobacco smoke, it all came flooding back in vivid detail.

It was a calm, cold day. Thaw had again given way to winter.

Cup of hot coffee clasped in both hands, he wondered what he should do. There was no longer any work, and there probably wouldn't be, the Chief having done a bunk. He had money for the time being, though he was $800 down. So, back to short stories perhaps, or maybe a novel . . .

As he attempted to divert himself with thoughts of future

prose, he had a sudden sense of emptiness. His prose was, in fact, all in a distant past – a past so distant as to raise a doubt as to whether it was *his* past at all. And not perhaps something read and forgotten, that now seemed part of what he had himself experienced.

Gulping his coffee, he remembered that Nina would be bringing Sonya back towards evening. Reality was asserting itself over his thoughts. What lay ahead was simply life as before: his duty to Sonya, care of Misha. Then, in all likelihood, a search for new employment . . . And solitude, as before.

He thought suddenly of Nina and her saying that they had been seeing Sergey off at the station. So he had, after all, gone to Moscow, and without so much as a goodbye. Another brick in Viktor's wall of solitude. And back to Nina. Nina of the half-smile, unsightly teeth and beautiful eyes. What colour they were, he couldn't recall.

But why think of her? He looked out of the window again. Fresh frost patterns were appearing on the glass. He would soon be 40, and the one creature closest to him was Penguin Misha – who had nowhere else to go, and being, moreover, denied the power of thought, was unable to contribute to the matter . . . And there was Sonya, not in the picture at all, with her pile of money and calm *The telly's mine!* Which, indeed, it was. And were they – he, Sonya and Misha, the four of them, including Nina – to go for a walk, someone would say *What a happy family!*

He smiled sadly, toying in imagination with happy illusions, real enough, from one point of view, to justify actually sitting for a family photograph.

48

Nina brought Sonya at six. She wanted to be off immediately, but Viktor asked her to join them for supper, and quickly boiled some potatoes.

Sonya behaved badly, and left the kitchen having eaten hardly anything.

Viktor and Nina ate on in silence, stealing the odd glance at each other.

"Has Sergey gone for long?" he asked.

"For a year, he said, but he's promised to come for a couple of days in the summer. His mother's still here. I'm doing her shopping for her now."

"What's she like? Old?"

"No, but her legs are bad."

They drank tea, and then Nina thanked him for the supper and said goodbye until tomorrow.

After seeing her out, Viktor went into the living room. The television was on and Sonya was asleep on the sofa, still dressed.

Tired out, he thought.

He undressed her and covered her with a blanket. As he went over to switch off the television, he saw penguins jumping comically from an iceberg into the water, all to a quiet commentary concerning Antarctic fauna.

He looked round for Misha, picked him up from where he was standing by the balcony door, and set him down in front of the TV.

Misha muttered.

"Watch," whispered Viktor.

Seeing his fellows, Misha stood gazing raptly at the screen.

For some five minutes they watched penguins jumping and diving, and when the programme ended, Misha shot over to the set and banged his chest against it, rocking it on its little table.

"Hey! You mustn't do that," Viktor said quietly, steadying the set.

Next morning the hospital rang.

"Your relative has died," announced a calm female voice.

"When?"

"In the night. Will you be collecting the body?"

Viktor said nothing.

"Will you be burying him?"

"Yes," he sighed.

"We can hold him in the mortuary for up to three days," said the voice, "while you organize the funeral. Don't forget to bring identification when you come to collect."

He replaced the receiver. He looked round at Sonya, no longer asleep but looking drowsily out from under the blanket.

The clock showed 8.30.

"You can sleep on for a bit," he said, leaving the room.

At 10.00 Nina arrived, and as she had a bit of a cold, said they would be staying in for the day.

"Any idea where scientists get buried?"

"The Baykov."

Dressed extra warmly against the cold, Viktor set off for the Baykov.

At the cemetery office, he was received by a fat elderly lady in a red woollen cardigan, sitting at an ancient desk and clasping in both hands a pair of pebble-lensed spectacles. Circumventing the centrally placed heater, he sat down opposite her and she put on her spectacles.

"A relative of mine has died," he began, "a scientist."

"Right," she said calmly. "Academician?"

"No."

"Any relatives buried here?"

"I don't know."

"So you'll need an individual plot," she said, mainly to herself, and opening a fat notebook lying on the desk, wrote something on a page and pushed it over.

Drawing the book towards him, Viktor read $1,000.

"Price of plot," she said, lowering her voice, "inclusive of special bus and gravedigging . . . It is, as you know, winter, and the ground's frozen solid."

"Right," he said.

"Name of deceased?"

"Pidpaly."

"Bring the money tomorrow, and the funeral's the day after, at eleven. Call here first, and I'll tell the driver the number of the plot. You can, incidentally, order a monument here."

49

The next day seemed to Viktor the most difficult of his life, but not from his having spent it organizing the funeral, because he hadn't. Emma Sergeyevna, mistress of obsequies at the Baykov, had produced a sheet clearly detailing the order of events:

11am., meet Special Bus number 66–77, at October Hospital Mortuary where Deceased, prepared by Funeral

Cosmetician ($100 extra), will await embusment. Deceased to repose in own attire in inexpensive quality pine casket.

Money had relieved Viktor of bother, but not of what weighed on his mind. He was in no mood to return to the flat – Nina and Sonya were there. He had told Nina that morning that a friend of his had died, and she had responded sympathetically, saying she would stay until he returned.

But instead of returning, he went to Podol, and sat at *Bacchus*'s until closing time, drinking three glasses of red wine. From the warmth of *Bacchus*'s he wandered around Podol until the cold got the better of him.

He reached the flat at about nine.

"I've made some soup – like me to heat it for you?" asked Nina.

After supper he asked her to stay, and she did.

With Sonya asleep in the living room, Viktor held Nina close to him in the bedroom. In spite of the two blankets over them, he still felt cold. Only in pressing close to her was there any warmth, though he was riled by the pitying look in her eyes. He tightened his grip, compressing her ribs, trying to hurt her, but she said nothing, just looked pityingly. She had her arms around him – he could feel her hands on his back – but her hold had something submissive and lacking in strength about it, as if she was simply hanging on to him. And just as submissively, she gave herself to him, saying nothing, uttering no sound. Still he had the urge to hurt, make her cry out and stop him, but soon wearied after achieving none of these things. Relaxing his embrace, he lay, eyes closed but not sleeping, unable to bear her pitying expression. He felt ashamed now – of himself, his fury,

127

his irritation, his grossness. And when at last he fell asleep, she lay for a long while, open-eyed, gazing at him and thinking – perhaps of the ability to endure.

When he woke next morning, she was no longer beside him. Fearing she might have gone, and for good, he got up, put on his dressing-gown and looked into the living room.

Sonya was still asleep. Hearing a sound in the kitchen, he found Nina, dressed and standing at the stove, boiling rice. He felt the need to say something, perhaps apologize. Turning, she nodded a greeting.

"I'm sorry," he whispered, gently embracing her.

Stretching up on tiptoe, she kissed him on the lips.

"When do you have to go?" she asked.

"At ten."

50

The funeral bus jolted mercilessly. The driver tried to drive slowly, but flashy foreign-made cars, in a hurry as always, kept sounding their horns, causing him to keep an anxious eye on his rear-view mirror.

In front sat two intelligent-looking little men, one wearing a short sheepskin coat, the other a black leather jacket, both 50-ish. One was the cosmetician, the other the undertaker, but which was which Viktor didn't know, since they had appeared simultaneously, helping the mortuary orderlies carry out the coffin and shove it through the rear door of the bus.

Viktor sat at the back with an arm around Misha to keep him

in his seat. Beside them, creaking as they rounded corners, was the coffin, nailed shut and covered with red and black material.

From time to time he met the inquisitive gaze of the little men, though it was Misha, not him, who was the object of their curiosity.

Arriving at the Baykov Cemetery, they stopped outside the office. The driver went to ask the plot number, and Viktor used this time to buy a large bunch of flowers from one of the old women standing there.

The way through the cemetery avenues seemed surprisingly long, and Viktor found the endless succession of monuments and railings wearying.

The bus stopped.

Viktor got up, preparing to make for the door.

"Not yet," said the driver, poking his head round the transparent partition.

"Look at that lot! Watch you don't scrape them!" said one of the little men, gazing ahead.

Viktor looked too. The right-hand side of the avenue was lined with flashy foreign-made cars, leaving a tight squeeze for the bus.

"Best make a detour," said the driver. "Out of harm's way."

They reversed and turned off into another avenue. Five minutes or so later they drew up at a newly dug grave. To one side was a heap of brown clayey soil and a couple of muddy spades.

Viktor got out. Surveying the scene, he saw a crowd of people about 50 metres away, and from the opposite direction, two skinny-looking cemetery hands in quilted jackets and trousers, both full of holes, were approaching.

"This the scientist?" asked one.

"Let's have him then," said the other with a jerk of the head.

They lowered the coffin to the ground beside the grave. One fetched a coil of stout rope and arranged it for the lowering of the coffin.

Viktor slipped back to the bus, lifted Misha out, and set him down. The rope-arranger looked askance, but worked on.

"Poor sort of do, this, isn't it?" the other workman asked the driver. "No priest, no palaver."

The driver looked pointedly in Viktor's direction to shut him up.

Having lowered the coffin, the workmen turned expectantly to the man with the penguin.

Going to the graveside, Viktor dropped the flowers onto the coffin lid, followed by a handful of earth.

The workmen plied their spades and in ten minutes the grave was formed. They then went their way, each with a million tip in the inflated currency of the country, saying he should look them up in May, when the grave had settled. Cosmetician and undertaker departed in the bus, and Viktor, who had declined the offer of a lift to the entrance, was left alone with Misha.

Misha was standing stiffly by the grave, as though deep in thought, and looking across at the neighbouring funeral. Viktor found its intrusive noise more than a little irritating.

It was odd to be playing sole mourner. Where were the friends, the relatives? Or had Pidpaly outlived them? More than likely. And, but for Viktor's interest in penguins, who would there have been to bury him, and where?

Cheeks nipped by the cold, gloveless hands freezing, he looked about him. He had no idea how to find his way out, but he wasn't worried.

"Well Misha," he sighed, stooping to the penguin's level, "that's how we humans bury our dead."

Turning at the sound of his master's voice, Misha fixed on him his tiny sad eyes.

"So, shall we look for the exit?" Viktor asked, and taking a more determined look around, saw a man heading towards them from the other funeral.

The man waved, and since there was no one else for him to wave at, Viktor stood and waited.

The man was short, bearded, and had binoculars slung about his *Alaska* anorak. Strange attire for a funeral, but his face seemed vaguely familiar.

"Sorry," he said. "But checking this sector" – he patted his binoculars – "and spying an animal known to me, I thought I'd pop over. New Year. Militia dachas. Remember?"

Viktor nodded.

"Lyosha," the bearded man said, extending his hand.

"Viktor."

They shook hands.

"Friend of yours?" Lyosha asked, indicating the grave.

"Yes."

"We're burying three," he sighed sadly.

Squatting down in front of Misha, he slapped him on the shoulder.

"Hi, Penguin. How are you doing? Afraid I've forgotten his name," he said, looking up.

"Misha."

"Ah, that's it, Misha! Bird in a suit . . . Handsome fellow!"

Straightening up, Lyosha looked back at his funeral.

"Do you know the way out?" Viktor asked.

Lyosha looked around.

"I don't . . . But if you're not in any hurry, hang on and I'll

131

give you a lift. We've nearly finished over there. The priest's a bore – half an hour's Bible over each one . . . You wait here – I'll give a wave when we're through."

Some 20 minutes later, Viktor saw movement in the crowd of mourners. They were dispersing. The flashy foreign-made cars were starting up. He looked hard for the bearded Lyosha, but having no binoculars, found his eyes watering from the icy wind. At last he saw someone waving.

"Come on, Misha," he said, taking a few steps and looking back, and slowly Misha followed.

By the time they arrived at the three wreath-heaped graves, only one car, an elderly Mercedes, was left.

"I'll drive you home if you like," said Lyosha, while still negotiating the cemetery. "Never does to be first at the wake."

Viktor readily accepted, and half an hour later was outside his block.

"Take my phone number – maybe we'll meet again," said Lyosha handing him his card. "And let me have yours, just in case."

Pocketing the card, Viktor wrote his number on the dashboard notepad.

51

Towards evening Nina made ready to leave.

"Won't you stay?" Viktor asked. "For the funeral supper."

He looked weary, and sounded unsure of himself. She nodded.

"You go and sit with Sonya – I'll think what to eat," she said. He went into the living room where Sonya had already switched the television on. Nina headed for the kitchen.

"What's it today?" he asked, sitting beside Sonya.

"*Elvira*, episode five," was the ready reply.

Taking out his handkerchief, he wiped her nose.

A lengthy commercial break was in progress. To spare his eyes the short sharp kaleidoscopic flashes, he looked at the floor, while Sonya feasted on them.

Eventually the frantic succession of commercials finished, to be followed by the serial credits and an enervating torrent of sickly music.

"Wouldn't you like to go to bed?" he asked.

"No," said the little girl, eyes riveted on the screen. "Would you?"

He said nothing. The treacly sweet Latin-Americanness of the characters was beginning to irritate him. He had no wish to enter into what was happening on the screen. He looked around for Misha, but he wasn't there. He was in the bedroom, standing still as a statue in his hidey-hole behind the dark-green settee. Viktor squatted down beside him.

"How are we?" he asked, patting a black shoulder.

Misha gave him a look, then stared at the floor.

Viktor found himself thinking of Pidpaly – how he had shaved him, what the old man had asked him to do, and how he had promised to do it, a memory he at once shelved, though with a shiver running down his spine.

Result of standing about at the cemetery, he thought.

He remembered how lightly, and without posture, the old penguinologist had faced imminent death. *I've no unfinished business* he had said. Viktor shook his head in sheer amazement, at which Misha stepped back and eyed him in alarm.

And nor have I, he thought, though the falsity of this brought a guilty smile to his face.

He did in fact have business to finish, and even if he hadn't, was hardly likely to treat the approach of death so lightly. *A hard life is better than an easy death* he had once written in his notebook. It was a phrase he had taken pride in for a time, trotting it out when appropriate and when not, and then forgotten. And here it was years later, floating to the surface of his memory, after Pidpaly's words that had so affected him. Two men, different ages, different attitudes.

Seeing his master squatting motionless, lost in thought, Misha came and nuzzled his neck with his beak, a chilly show of tenderness that broke Viktor's train of thought and roused him from his reverie. He stroked the penguin, sighed, straightened up and went over to the window.

The block opposite presented a crossword pattern of lighted windows. It was a crossword with many spaces. They were testimonies to the sheer ordinariness of life, those windows. There was a sadness about it, but a sadness softened, allayed, by darkness. And by degrees, a strange, slightly unnatural calm, like the lull before a storm, possessed him. Palms resting on the cold window sill, legs against the hot radiator, he stood, aware how temporary it was, that calm, and waiting for it to pass.

A little later, at the sound of gentle breathing, he swung round, and there in the half-darkness was Nina.

"It's ready," she whispered. "Sonya's asleep – dropped off watching the telly."

They went through the living room, now dimly lit by a standard lamp in the corner.

The kitchen smelt of garlic and fried potato, and on a stand in the middle of the table reposed the covered frying pan.

"I saw you had some vodka," Nina ventured, indicating the wall cupboard. "Shall I bring it?"

He nodded. She fetched the bottle and two small glasses, served the meat and fried potatoes, and filled their glasses.

Viktor sat in his place, Nina opposite.

"How was the funeral?" she asked.

"Quiet. No one there, except Misha and me."

"Well, may he rest in peace!" She raised her glass before putting it to her lips.

Viktor drank too. He cut up his meat, and looking across at Nina, saw a round face all the more charming for the flush the vodka had brought to it.

He knew nothing about her, he thought suddenly, who she was, where she was from. Niece of Sergey, yes, but what did he know about him, beyond that he had been easy to make friends with. The origin of his name had been enough to engender a warm feeling towards him. The story of that seemed to set him on an invisible pedestal, elevate him to a point where delight in the man was sufficient to inspire complete confidence.

Viktor poured refills and raised his glass.

"Did you know him well?" Nina asked.

Viktor drank.

"I think so."

"What was he?"

"A scientist. Worked at the zoo."

She nodded, but with an expression showing plainly that interest in the deceased was now terminated.

They ate, and in deference to the occasion, drank without clinking glasses. Nina then placed their dirty plates in the sink and put the kettle on. Waiting for it to boil, she looked out of the window, face contorted, as if in pain.

"What's wrong?"

"It's this city, I can't stand it . . . The anonymous crowds . . . The distances . . ."

"But why?" He asked in surprise.

Thrusting her hands in the pockets of her jeans, she shrugged.

"My fool of a mother threw everything over, and moved here . . . I wouldn't have! Your own place with your own little garden. All yours. That's what's best."

Viktor sighed. Being city-born, he had no special feeling for the country.

The kettle boiled.

Again they sat opposite each other, separated by silence, thinking their own thoughts.

Feeling sleepy, Viktor got to his feet, surprised at the heaviness of his legs.

"I'm off to bed."

"Off you go. I'll wash up."

Once in bed he fell instantly asleep. Waking in the small hours because he was hot, he became aware of another warmth, that of Nina sleeping with her back to him.

Placing a hand on her shoulder, he fell asleep again, satisfied, as if his doubts were dispelled, and the hand on her shoulder was a channel of vital warmth between them, precious, and no obstacle to slumber.

52

And again it was morning. Viktor woke with a heavy head and no Nina beside him. The clock showed 8.30.

He made his way through the living room, where Sonya was still asleep, to the kitchen. He could hear water splashing in the bathroom.

As he went to the stove to make coffee, he caught sight of an envelope on the table. It was sealed, but bore no name. Tearing it open, he extracted a folded sheet of paper and eight $100 notes.

> Debt repaid with thanks. Things
> on the mend. Back soon. – Igor.

Viktor dropped the sheet on the table, keeping hold of the dollars.

He looked into the bathroom. Nina was under the shower, the smooth lines of her body emphasized by the flow of water. Seeing him standing stiffly in the doorway, she was more surprised than embarrassed.

"Has anyone been?" he asked.

"No," she said, staring at the dollar bills in his hand.

"How about the letter on the kitchen table?"

"I haven't been in there yet." She said, shrugging so that her tiny apple breasts quivered.

Shutting the bathroom door, he stood in the corridor, trying to concentrate, but distracted by the splashing. He thought back to all that had happened the evening before, to everything Nina had said at table. After which he had gone to bed, and now, next morning, evidence of a visitor. No marks on the floor, but the evidence remained . . .

At this point he switched on the corridor light and examined the floor for traces of the night visitor or visitors, but there were none.

Returning to the kitchen, he made coffee and sat down at the table. He remembered his discovery of Misha-non-penguin's note and presents before New Year. This was an exact repeat – only this time, with delivery of a letter from the Chief in place of presents. *Things on the mend* . . . Did that mean there would soon be work? That he would soon be seeing the Chief and could ask what sort of postal service it was that had keys to his flat?

Keys . . . He got up, went and tried the door. It was tight shut. He returned to the kitchen.

He could, he comforted himself, replace the lock. There had long been plenty to choose from: alarmed, coded, electrically controlled . . . He might even get a couple of combination locks. His flat, personal life and sleep would then be totally secure.

Reassured, he brewed coffee for Nina, and was taking it to her when he met her coming in. She was wearing his dressing-gown.

"Just made you some coffee," he said.

"Thanks," she smiled, took the cup and sat down at the table.

"Vik," her expression now was half-serious, half-entreating. "What I wanted to say . . ." she hesitated, as if choosing her words. "Well, it's about us . . . Now we've somehow become a couple . . ."

She fell silent.

"How do you mean?" he asked, filled with unease at the ensuing pause.

"It's my wages," she said at last. "It means a lot to me . . . The money I get for Sonya."

"Of course, and you'll still get it," he said in surprise. "What made you think you wouldn't?"

She shrugged.

"Don't you see, it's a bit awkward – our being a couple, and me working for you at the same time."

The heavy head he had banished with his first cup of coffee was suddenly back.

"It's all right," he said gravely. "Don't worry – it's not me who's paying. It's Sonya – it's her father's money."

Embarrassed, Nina sat staring at the table and the coffee cup before her.

"Don't worry," he said, getting up and smoothing her wet hair. "It's all right."

She nodded, but did not look up.

"I'll be back late," he said. "Don't open to anyone. And here's something in advance . . ."

He put two green $100 bills on the table, and left.

53

Before taking the Metro to Svyatoshino, Viktor wandered the city for a while. After several clearly fortuitous thaws, February had turned sharp again. The sun shone, the snow sparkled underfoot, and his hands were like ice in the pockets of his short sheepskin coat. Clutched, no less ice-cold, in his right hand, were the keys to Pidpaly's flat.

This time, the cold lending wings to his feet, it took him about ten minutes to walk from the Metro to Pidpaly's flat. Quickly letting himself in, he stamped the snow off his feet and went through to the kitchen. It was tidy, and only the combination of damp and stuffiness recalled the day when the ambulance he had summoned carried Pidpaly off for ever.

Something in the air made him sneeze.

He would have done better to die at home, he thought, gazing round at the ancient kitchen furniture, the stopped clock, the terracotta ashtray on the window ledge, obviously never used, either because the old man had forgotten about it or because he wished to keep it safe.

He entered the living room. Old-fashioned chairs were drawn up to the round table. A chandelier with five frosted-glass shades hung from the centre of the ceiling. Facing the door was a chest of drawers supporting three towering bookshelves. The books were concealed behind photographs and newspaper cuttings. There were also photographs on the walls, framed and redolent of the past. The whole furnishing of the flat was of a past age.

It reminded Viktor of the flat of the grandmother who had brought him up after his parents divorced and went their separate ways. Part of an old house in Tarasov Street, that had been old-fashioned too, in some respects, though he had paid no heed to it at the time. There had been a chest of drawers there, as well, only smaller, and standing on it a glass cabinet displaying Granny's proudest possessions: the china vases presented to her for her achievements at work. There were five or six of them, each bearing her name and initials, the date, and a brief account of the occasion, neatly and painstakingly inscribed in gold ink. And there had been the same framed photographs of the same epoch, that same recent but already so far distant past of a country that no longer existed.

He went over to the chest of drawers. In the bookcase photographs he recognized Pidpaly – with a woman, against a background of palms, and underneath was *Yalta, Summer 1960*. He looked closely – Pidpaly was then 40, 45, and the permed lady evidently of similar age. In another photograph Pidpaly was standing alone beside a swimming pool out of which a dolphin poked its head. *Batumi, Summer 1981* ran the legend.

The past believed in dates. And everyone's life consisted of dates, giving life a rhythm and sense of gradation, as if from the eminence of a date one could look back and down, and see the past itself. A clear, comprehensible past, divided up into squares of events, lines of paths taken.

Here, despite the odour of damp books, and perhaps by virtue of being on the ground floor, he felt at ease and safe. These walls with their faded paper, the dust-laden shades of the chandelier, the rows of photographs, had something of a mesmerizing effect.

He sat down at the table, and again thought of his grandmother, Aleksandra Vasilyevna, who, when she was old, used to take a little stool and sit outside the block. *God grant I'm never paralysed*, she would say, *it'd ruin your life and lose you a wife!* He had laughed, but Granny, decrepit as she was, had wormed out of her neighbours the phone number of a flat-fixer. Two months later Viktor had a two-room flat, and Granny had moved to a ground-floor one-roomer in a Khrushchev slum, where, quietly, virtually unnoticed, she died. Social Security buried her, and her neighbours gave three roubles each towards a wreath. All of which Viktor had learnt six months later, returning home from the army.

Feeling like a cup of tea, he went to the kitchen. Darkness was falling. As he switched on the light, the ancient refrigerator rumbled into life. Surprised, he took a look inside. Green sausage, and an open tin of condensed milk. He took out the milk, and in the tall, narrow kitchen cupboard found a packet of tea.

His sensation of comfort, albeit someone else's, was mixed with unease. He drank the tea, eating solidified condensed milk with it. The voices of people walking by outside alternated with the noise of a passing car.

Feeling a tickle in his throat, he poured himself a second cup, drank it, and returning to the living room, switched on the light. He looked into the study – all bookshelves and bookcases – went over to the desk, and lighting the table lamp, also ancient and with a marble base, sat down on the black leather chair.

The desk was scattered with notebooks. Noticing a thick diary beside the lamp, he leafed through it – pages of hurried minuscule handwriting interspersed with paper markers. The diary opened by itself at one such marker – a newspaper cutting. He moved closer to the light. It reported Britain's gift to Ukraine of a station in the Antarctic. The report ended with an appeal for sponsors, *without whose financial support it would not be possible to send Ukrainian scientists there.* A telephone number was given for inquiries, and a bank account number for donations.

What, wondered Viktor, had the Antarctic to do with Ukraine?

There was, he saw also, a receipt in respect of a postal draft. Examining it, he almost doubted his sanity. Pidpaly had sent the Antarctic Appeal five million, in the grossly inflated national currency, probably the pathetic total of his savings.

Putting receipt and cutting aside, he studied the old man's notes, but could decipher only a few odd words. Pidpaly's thoughts were encoded and inaccessible to the outsider, by virtue of his writing.

Again he had a sense of unease and an itching in his fingertips, as though from contact with something incomprehensible, inexplicable.

He had not forgotten his promise to the old man, but preferred for the moment not to think about it. And although he had come not thinking about it, it was after all what had drawn him there, the cold keys in his cold hand guiding him like a compass.

And here he sat amid things and papers that were no longer anybody's – in a whole world left without its creator and master. The old man had wanted no outsiders to have contact with it, or to see the destruction of a cosy little world three or four decades behind the times.

He gave a deep sigh and had a sudden urge to pull out the desk drawers or rummage in the chest of drawers in search of something to salvage as a memento. But the frozen integrity, the immobility of Pidpaly's little world prevented him. He sat contemplating the cutting and receipt, the diary and other notebooks.

The street was silent now, and the combined silence of street and flat stirred him into action. He put the newspaper cutting in his jacket pocket.

He looked round at the study walls, but didn't touch anything else. He fetched matches from the gas stove in the kitchen. In a small wall cupboard in the corridor he found a bottle of acetone, which he took back to the study. Closing his mind to what he was doing, he splashed acetone over the books on the lower shelves and on a pile of old newspapers under the desk. Half the pile of newspapers he took into the living room and put under the dinner table, throwing the tea-stained cloth to join them. He then went around setting light to the papers and anything that would burn. Flames hissed in both rooms, but as yet too feebly to engulf that doomed world. Discovering sheets, pillowcases and towels in the chest of drawers, he added them to the blaze, together with Pidpaly's raincoat from its peg in the corridor.

In a whirl of black smuts, the air grew hotter, filling the room with smoke and sparks and forcing him out into the corridor.

The crackle of burning grew steadily louder. Flames had already penetrated the table top and were now licking at the legs.

Feeling for Pidpaly's keys, he made for the door, but darted back to switch off the living room light. The fire glowed a deeper red in the dark, more beautiful and terrible than before.

He locked the outer door behind him.

He made a circuit of the block, then stopped opposite Pidpaly's windows and watched the flames shooting up to the ceiling. He looked up at the first floor. No lights were showing – the people there were either asleep or not yet back.

He took another look through the window at the dancing flames.

So that was that. He had kept his promise.

But his hands were shaking and cold shivers were running up and down his spine.

Turning away, he spotted a telephone at the corner of the neighbouring block, and from here he called the fire brigade.

Glass shattered, as if the fire were forcing its way out. A woman screamed. Five minutes later he heard the wail of fire-engine sirens. With two appliances on the scene and their crews bustling about, rolling out hoses and shouting. Viktor took a last look at the now doomed flames, and set off at an unhurried pace to the Metro.

He had the taste of smoke in his mouth. Snowflakes fell lightly on his face, but before they could melt, were blown away by an icy wind.

54

"Your hair smells of bonfire," Nina whispered sleepily as Viktor slipped into bed.

He muttered some reply, turned away and fell asleep immediately, totally exhausted.

He woke at about ten, hearing Sonya conversing with Misha beside the bed.

"Sonya, where's Auntie Nina?"

"Gone. We had breakfast and then she went. We've left you something."

On the kitchen table he found two boiled eggs and under the salt cellar, a note:

Hi! Didn't want to wake you. Going to give Sergey's mother a hand: shop and do the washing. Be back the moment I've finished. Love, Nina.

Screwing up the note, Viktor felt the eggs. They were cold. He made himself some tea and breakfasted.

He went back to the bedroom.

"Fed Misha, Sonya?"

"Yes. He's had two fish today, but he still seems unhappy.

Why, Uncle Vik?"

He perched on the settee.

"I don't know," he said with a shrug. "I think they're only happy in cartoons."

"All animals are, in cartoons," Sonya said with an airy wave of the hand.

He noticed, looking at her, that she was wearing a new emerald-coloured dress.

"That's new, isn't it?"

"Present from Nina. Yesterday on our walk we went into a shop . . . That's where she gave it to me. Pretty, isn't it?"

"Yes."

"The penguin likes it, too."

"You've asked him, have you?"

"Yes. But he's not happy. Maybe it's bad for him here."

"That's probably it," he agreed. "What he likes is cold, and here it's warm."

"Perhaps we could put him in the fridge."

He looked at Misha standing beside her, rocking slightly on his feet, chest rising with each breath.

"We mustn't do that – he'd be too cramped, you see. I expect he wants to go home, but home's a long way away."

"Very, very far?"

"The Antarctic."

"Where's that?"

"Think of the earth as round. Can you do that?"

"Like a ball? Yes, I can."

"Well, we're standing on the top, and penguins live at the bottom, almost underneath us . . ."

"With their feet in the air?"

146

"In a way, yes. But we seem to them to have our feet in the air when they think of it . . . Do you see?"

"Yes," she declared loudly. "And I can stand with my legs in the air!"

And resting her back against the edge of the settee, she had a go at standing on her head, but couldn't keep it up.

"But I *can* do it," she said, sitting down on the carpet again. "It's just that I'm heavier after breakfast."

He smiled. This was the first time in these several months that he had chatted with Sonya so easily and without secret irritation, and it seemed strange. For he had not lost the feeling of Sonya's being someone else's and accidental to his own life. She had, so to speak, been dumped on him, and he had been too good-natured to take her to wherever dumped children get taken. Of course, it hadn't been quite like that. He had been guided by an odd sense of duty towards her. It was to him that Misha-non-penguin, whom he had hardly known, had entrusted her when danger threatened. Had he lived, he would have come and collected her. But now there was no one to come. Misha-non-penguin had made no mention of Sonya's mother. Friend-enemy Sergey Chekalin's half-hearted, half-cock attempt to take her had ended in his making off without a word. And now, here was Sonya at home in his flat, and not being specially disturbing or tiresome. Thanks, it was true, to Nina, who, but for Sonya, would never have come on the scene. In which case he and Misha would have gone on as before, and life would have been neither bad nor good, just ordinary.

Nina arrived at about three. From Sergey's mother's she had gone back to the shops, and now unpacked curds for Sonya, frankfurters, cottage cheese . . .

"Do you know," she said, as Viktor came into the kitchen, "Sergey rang today from Moscow. He's OK."

She kissed him.

"And you still smell of bonfire!" she added, with a smile.

55

Several days passed. Quiet, monotonous days. Viktor's sole activity during this time was the changing of the two door locks. He did the buying and changing himself. The feeling of satisfaction lasted several hours, but then boredom set in again. He had to do something, but there was nothing to do. And he didn't feel like writing.

"Uncle Vik!" Sonya cried delightedly, standing at the balcony window. "The icicles are crying!"

The thaw was back. And not before time – it was the beginning of March.

He was waiting for spring, as if warmth might prove the solution to all his problems. Although when he actually fell to thinking about his problems, he realized that he had practically none as such. He had money for the moment, especially since the Chief's mysterious night-mail repayment. And up on the wardrobe, in a bag together with the revolver, there was still a good fat bundle of $100 notes, which, though they were Sonya's, he had a moral right to a share of as her unofficial guardian.

As before, Nina kept Sonya amused during the day, sometimes at home, sometimes out and about, leaving Viktor on his own. But at night they were reunited, and knowing that neither love nor passion came into it, he still found arms and body anticipating that time with eagerness. Embracing, caressing Nina, making love, he became oblivious of himself. The warmth of her body seemed to be that very spring he so looked forward to. And then, in the small hours, with Nina asleep and breathing gently, he lay open-eyed, with the curiously comfortable sensation of leading an ordered, normal life – for which the essential requisites: wife, child, pet penguin, were present; and obviously artificial as this foursome was, Viktor shut his eyes to this fact for the sake of his feeling of comfort and a temporary illusion of happiness. But who could say? Maybe his happiness was not as illusory as the sober thoughts of morning suggested. But what, at night, were the thoughts of the morning? The very alternation of nocturnal happiness with morning common sense, and the constancy of it, seemed to prove that he was, at one and the same time, both happy and clear-thinking. So that all was well and life worth living.

Just as he was fetching Misha's breakfast from the freezer, the phone rang. He threw the slices of fish into the bowl and went and picked up the receiver in the living room.

"Greetings!" came a familiar voice. "How's life?"

"Fine."

"I'm back in Kiev," said the voice, now clearly the Chief's. "You can consider your holiday at an end."

"Shall I come and see you?"

"Why waste time? I'll send a courier. Give him the finished work, he'll give you the new. Will you be in?"

"Yes."

"Splendid! Incidentally, it's a paid holiday you've just had, although not a union member. Bye!"

Viktor made coffee, rejoicing in the peace of the flat – Nina and Sonya having gone to Pushcha-Voditsa to look for snowdrops. A peace which enabled him to sit down with a cup of coffee and calmly think it all over. A peace which made it possible to sit without thinking even, just drinking coffee, dwelling on its flavour, keeping at arm's length thoughts capable of disturbing equanimity.

But sitting sipping strong coffee, he felt suddenly on edge, and as Misha dropped a piece of fish, he gave a start and swung round to look.

The flavour of coffee became of secondary importance. His edginess increased. Disquieting thoughts prompted an onslaught of questions.

What now? Back to *obelisks*? Back to red-underlined biographical facts of people unaware that their obituaries were already in hand? Occasional coffee-drinking sessions in the Chief's sanctum? The Chief's kindly attitude, the shaky roundness of his handwriting? His laconic brevity, his attachment to that one word *processed*, entered repeatedly, neatly, painstakingly on the originals of *obelisks* which had already informed readers of the terminated life of whoever was next to merit an extensive obituary?

This new genre, his invention, lived. Unlike so many of its subjects. But no longer did he yearn for recognition or feel an urge to shout *I wrote that!* The anonymity of *A Group of Friends* suited him completely. The Group, he sensed, was not just him alone. The Chief was one of the Friends, too. And there was another, the Principal Friend perhaps, that someone whose bold, sweeping signature approved Viktor's *obelisks*. Though whether it was the text he approved or the subject, was now not at all clear. And then there were the dates, obviously determining the day

150

of publication, but clearly predetermined during the subject's lifetime! Death as *planned economy!*

No, it was not the quality of his text, his philosophical digressions, or felicitous presentation of U-turns in the lives of his notables that this someone was approving, but the notables themselves – determining how long they had left to live. And the Chief's role in all this was a surprisingly minor one – a peculiar cross between courier and ticket inspector. And although his duties certainly included publishing *obelisks* on schedule, even that did not now seem particularly significant – any more than his own role, which Viktor still did not completely understand.

Out of the blue, and contrary to this logical line of thought, he remembered something that diverted him from it and made his blood run cold. And just as he seemed about to grasp what was going on, he was back where he started, with his attempt to solve an equation having two knowns and one unknown frustrated. What he had remembered was how the Chief had responded to his probing on the night when the car had been waiting to take him to the airport: *The full story is what you get told only if and when your work, and with it your existence, are no longer required.*

It had seemed then that he and the Chief were parting for ever. And Viktor had naturally thought that his work was now at an end, although the mystery unearthed in the Chief's safe continued to disquiet him. But by the next day it was as if time had relegated that to the distant past. And the time distance created in imagination between past mystery and a Viktor now entering upon a new stage of existence, blunted interest in the former, regardless of his own obvious involvement. Better, he thought, not to know, yet still be alive – especially as it was now all over and done with.

And now it turned out that far from over and done with, it

was still going on, with him still working, still paying especial attention to underlinings in red.

Was it worth trying to discover *what* was going on? Worth risking comfort – curious though it might be – and peace of mind? He would still have to write *obelisks*, still have to be needed in order to stay alive.

Again the Chief's parting shot came to mind.

To hell with it, Viktor decided. Easier all round not to give it a thought.

Picking up the long-completed batch of military *obelisks* from the window ledge, he ran through the names and what he had written.

What difference did it make to him what happened to these generals? Or for what date some unknown person had planned their deaths and subsequent obituaries, the latter suggestive of their richly deserving to die?

If then his life was that dependent on his work, let that work continue. In which case it might be best simply to distance himself from what was going on. Not do anything foolish, like trying to disappear or lose himself in some other city – but, more simply: realize Nina's dream – buy a little house in the country, move and live happily there, all four of them together, he writing his *obelisks* and sending them off to the city, as one might to another land where not all was as it should be.

Out of which thoughts he was jolted by Misha laying his head upon his knee, and looking down at the penguin, he stroked him.

"How about a move to the country?" he asked Misha, smiling wrily at the apparent unreality of his dreams.

56

As if to confirm yesterday as indeed the end of his holiday, Viktor sat now at his typewriter, sipping hot coffee and contemplating the new *obelisk* laboriously taking shape. The other half of the kitchen table was occupied by Sonya with her pencils and felt-tipped pens, Nina having gone somewhere that morning, leaving no note. But he wasn't worried – she wouldn't be long.

In the folder of new material brought by courier the evening before, as well as files on a number of representatives of the Ministry of Health, he had found an envelope of *holiday pay*. At least, those were the words typed on the slip of paper accompanying the $500. Money which gave a little lift to his creative spirit. Even so, progress was terribly slow. Words refused to deploy in battle formation, sentences scattered, only to be slaughtered by irritable x's and reformed.

"Is it like him?" Sonya asked suddenly, showing her drawing.

He looked closely. "What's it supposed to be?"

"Misha!"

He shook his head.

"It looks," he said thoughtfully, "more like a chicken."

Sonya frowned, looked at the drawing, and threw it on the floor.

"No good being cross," he coaxed. "Learn drawing from life is what you've got to do."

"How?"

"Just sit down in front of Misha, look at him, and draw. That'll make it like him."

Pleased with this idea, she gathered up pencils and felt tips,

153

got a few more sheets of paper from Viktor, and set off in search of Misha.

Viktor went back to work. He managed, in the end, to get through the first *obelisk*, and having done so, massaged his temples. Clearly he was rusty.

A door banged.

Nina, he thought. The alarm clock on the window ledge showed just short of noon.

A minute later she looked into the kitchen.

"Hi!" She was all smiles.

His response was on the cold side.

"Notice anything?"

He looked. Same jeans, familiar sweater. No change.

He shrugged, looked at her, puzzled at first, then more closely.

"Well?" she urged, still smiling.

"Your teeth!" he exclaimed, astonished.

And it was – beautifully white, no trace of yellow. Hers was now the smile of the dentifrice advert.

He too smiled.

"At last!" She kissed him resoundingly on the cheek. "I had to wait a whole month. $400, and I could have had it done without waiting. I got it for $80 . . ."

Sonya came running in with a sheet of paper. "Nina, look! I've drawn Misha!"

She showed Nina, who squatted down, studied the drawing, and patted her on the back.

"Well done!" she said. "We'll frame it and hang it on the wall."

"Can we?" Sonya was delighted.

"Of course! So everyone can see it."

Viktor also had a look. Her drawing had caught something of the penguin.

"Right!" said Nina standing up. "I think we all deserve a good lunch today, so clear the kitchen!"

Sonya took her drawing to the living room, and Viktor followed.

Nina was already behaving like the lady of the house, he thought, but he was not the least bit angry. On the contrary, he was even cheered by the thought.

57

The first drizzle of spring was falling. The snow in the courtyard had almost all melted, and only under bushes were doomed remnants of winter still to be seen in the shape of frozen lumps. Another few days and fresh green blades of grass would peep from the warm soil.

Viktor was sitting at the kitchen table, chair turned to the window, a cup of tea forgotten and growing cold beside him, staring down at the courtyard. He was looking forward to the warmth of spring. And although it was hardly likely to change his life, a certain vague, in no way justified feeling of hope brought a smile of pleasure to his face, as he saw the sunlight shafting through a light mix of bright and dark cloud.

The latest batch of *obelisks* lay ready in their folder on the table. He could ring the Chief and say the job was done, or he could wait another day, putting off work on the next batch for a bit.

Shifting his thoughts from the rain, he wondered who the

next lot of *obelisk* notables would be. Cosmonauts? Submariners?

He had become accustomed to the files he received bringing together people already linked by interests or professions – military, health officials, State Deputies – and it no longer struck him as strange. The notebook he had opened when he started had lain forgotten since the Chief had called a halt to personal initiative in the choice of notables. After that, Viktor had given up reading papers in search of VIPs. He now worked exclusively on *semi-finished material*, in the form of detailed files. This was both easier and more suspicious. The more he worked, the more his suspicions grew, until they became the absolute certainty that this whole *obelisk* business was part of a patently criminal operation. The realization of this in no way influenced his daily life and work. And although he could not help thinking about it, he found it easier to do so every day, having recognized the complete impossibility of ever changing his life. Harnessed as he was, it was a question of hauling his load until he dropped. So he hauled.

The sitting-room phone rang, and the next moment Nina poked her head round the kitchen door.

"For you, Vik."

He went and picked up the receiver.

"That you, Vik?" an unknown man's voice enquired.

"Yes."

"It's me, Lyosha, remember? Gave you a lift from the cemetery."

"Ah, hello."

"Something rather important. I'll be outside your place in 20 minutes. Come down when you see me."

"Who was that?" Nina asked, seeing Viktor standing perplexed, still holding the receiver.

"Someone I know."

"Sonya and I are learning to read, aren't we, Sonya?"

"Yes," the little girl confirmed, sitting on the settee with a book.

Hearing a car draw up outside, Viktor put on his jacket and went down.

"Get in," said Lyosha.

The door banged shut. It was cold in the car.

"How's the animal?" Lyosha asked amiably, stroking his beard.

"All right."

"It's like this," his face grew serious. "I'd like to invite you and said animal to a certain occasion . . . Not exactly a jolly one, but there'll be money in it."

"What sort of occasion?" Viktor asked drily, becoming interested.

"The boss of some friends of mine has died. Funeral's tomorrow. A big affair, as you can imagine. Bronze-handled coffin – cost a packet. I'd told them about your penguin, and now they've remembered . . . You and he are invited."

"What for?" Viktor stared amazed.

"How shall I put it . . . " hesitant drawing in of lower lip. "A touch of style's called for . . . And to have a penguin there would supply it, they thought. With a vengeance. Naturally suited, isn't he, being black and white? . . . Get the idea?"

He did, though it all seemed like a stupid joke.

"Are you serious?" he asked, looking sharply at Lyosha and meeting an expression that was gravity itself.

"I'd call $1,000 for hire of a penguin serious," he replied, forcing a smile.

"I'm not too happy about it," Viktor confessed, finally convinced that Lyosha was serious.

157

"To be frank, you've no option," declared the bearded Lyosha. "It's an offer you can't refuse. The departed's friends could take it amiss . . . Don't make problems for yourself. I'll pick you up tomorrow about ten."

Viktor got out and watched until the car disappeared around the block, heading for the road.

Back in the flat he locked himself into the bathroom. While the water ran, he stood in front of the mirror, staring, as if at a photograph he wanted to remember.

58

Next day they drove to the Baykov Cemetery in Lyosha's ancient foreign-made car, Viktor and Misha in the back. They drove in silence.

At the cemetery entrance they were stopped by a young fellow in camouflage combat gear, who bent down at Lyosha's window, nodded, and waved him on.

Monuments, railings flitted past. Viktor felt fit for nothing.

The avenue ahead was blocked by a cortège of parked foreign-made cars.

"We'll have to walk a bit," said Lyosha, turning to Viktor in the back.

Taking binoculars from the glove compartment and slinging them around his neck, he got out.

The sky was cloudless, the sun shone, and the air was filled with inappropriately cheerful birdsong. Viktor looked about him.

They made their way slowly past the impressive, new, foreign-made cars to where a crowd of people were waiting.

"Why the binoculars?" Viktor asked as they walked.

Lyosha, slightly ahead of him, looked back.

"We all have our job to do. Mine is to provide protection and ensure order, so no one spoils the –" he stopped short – "so that everything's in order."

Viktor nodded.

The crowd of sombrely well-dressed men made way for them.

They stopped at the graveside by the open coffin, in which lay a man in his 40s, grey-haired and wearing gold-rimmed spectacles. His stylish suit was covered up to the chest with sprays of flowers.

A tense look around showed that Lyosha had vanished, and that he and Misha were surrounded by sombre-faced strangers, none of whom seemed to pay him or the penguin any attention whatever.

At the head of the coffin stood the priest, Bible open, muttering into his beard. Standing behind him was a young man in a cassock, who was evidently his curate.

Viktor would have liked to shut his eyes until all was over. But there was a kind of almost electric tension in the air that every now and then produced an unwelcome, yet annoyingly invigorating pricking sensation to face and hands. He stood, like the penguin, motionless. The burial ritual took its course. On the brow of the deceased was a strip of paper bearing a cross and an inscription in Old Church Slavonic. The priest opened his book at the next marker, and in a strained baritone, launched into his gloomy recitative. All bowed their heads, except Misha, who stood as before, head bent, gazing into the grave.

Viktor squinted down at him.

They were part of this ritual, Misha and he.

The coffin having been lowered on ropes by two spotlessly attired gravediggers, the mourners came back to life. Earth drummed down on the coffin lid.

And for the first time, Viktor and Misha seemed to attract interest to the extent of receiving oblique glances, of curiosity, perhaps, or sorrow.

"You're invited by the next of kin to join them at the wake," Lyosha announced, coming over to him. "Just you, not the animal. Six o'clock this evening. *Hotel Moscow* restaurant. And I've been given this for you."

He handed over an envelope which Viktor mechanically pocketed without a word.

"Go to the car. I'll catch you up," Lyosha added, slipping away.

Looking round, Viktor saw there was a little old man videoing the proceedings.

"Well, shall we go home?" he asked, squatting down in front of Misha, saddened by the indifference his eyes reflected.

They drove home. Again in silence.

"Don't forget the wake!" called Lyosha, as they parted.

Viktor nodded. The car drove off.

"To hell with the wake!" he thought, climbing the stairs with Misha in his arms.

59

With Sonya abed, Viktor and Nina sat in the kitchen that evening, drinking wine and talking. He gave her an account of the *funeral with penguin.*

"So what?" she asked skittishly. "For $1,000, why worry?"

For a minute he was silent, then he said, "I don't . . . It's a lot of money . . . Just that it's strange . . ."

"Maybe you'll raise my wages, now Misha's earning," she said, smiling but serious. And then in a gentler tone she added, "I'm always spending on our behalf anyway. I bought some little boots for Sonya . . ."

"For heaven's sake, don't call it wages," he said with a sigh. "I'll let you have some money in the morning. When that's gone just tell me."

He looked at her and shook his head.

"What is it?"

"Just that you're very much the country girl, sometimes."

"I was born in the country," she confirmed, smiling again.

"Right. Let's go to bed," he said, rising from the table.

Next morning he woke to find Nina shaking him.

"What is it?" he asked sleepily, and with no inclination to get up.

"In the kitchen, there's a bag." She was clearly worried. "Come and see."

Getting up, Viktor threw on a dressing-gown, and headed uncertainly for the kitchen.

There was indeed a bag on the table. Back to the old tricks, he thought wearily.

He went and checked the locks. The door was securely shut.

Returning to the kitchen, he gingerly felt the bag, and emboldened by the outline of a bottle, set about unpacking it.

Five minutes later, having examined the contents, he called Nina.

Nina came in, stopped dead, and gazed in amazement at what

161

was laid out on the table: a plate of fish in aspic, a clingfilm-covered restaurant selection of traditional meats, fresh tomatoes, a chop, a bottle of Smirnoff vodka.

"Where did this come from?"

Pulling a face, Viktor pointed to the blue letters forming the abbreviation of *Ukrainian Restaurants* on the rim of a plate.

"There's a note," Nina said, indicating the bottle.

Scotch-taped to the neck was a folded piece of paper which, detached and unfolded, read:

> Don't do that again, old chap. Respect for the dead! This
> is from the relatives. It's Aleksandr Safronov's memory
> you'll be drinking to.
>
> See you! – Lyosha.

"Who's it from?"

He handed her the note. She read it, then looked at him, perplexed.

"What was it you did?"

"I didn't go to the wake."

"You should have gone," she said quietly.

Giving her an irritable look, he went and felt in the pockets of his sheepskin jacket for Lyosha's card, and snatching up the receiver, dialled his number.

For a long time there was no response.

At long last a thick, sleepy voice said, "Hello?"

"Lyosha?" Viktor asked coldly.

Lyosha, clearly the worse for a night's drinking, muttered indistinctly.

"It's me, Vik. Look, about this stunt with the bag –"

"What stunt? Is it really you, Vik? How's the animal?"

"Listen, that bag, how did it get into my kitchen?" Viktor demanded irritably.

"*How?* By request of the next of kin . . . What's bugging you?"

"What's bugging me is how it got through closed doors!" His voice was now almost a shout.

"Take it easy. I hear you. But I've got a headache . . . *Through closed doors* – you ask? But no doors ever are completely closed! Grow up! Drink to Safronov's memory. Me, I've got to sober up, too, but I'd like a bit of sleep first. What the hell did you have to wake me for?"

He hung up.

Viktor shook his head, sick at heart at this evidence of his own impotence and defencelessness.

"Vik!" Nina called from the kitchen.

"Coming."

The table was already laid. Two plates had vodka glasses beside them.

"Why waste good stuff? When it's still fresh . . . Sit down. – Sonya!" she called into the corridor. "Come and eat. We must drink to this person – it's bad not to," she said, turning to Viktor, who was still standing by the table, and following the direction of her eyes, he unscrewed the Smirnoff bottle.

"Look what I've drawn!" said Sonya, coming in with a sheet of paper and holding it out to Nina.

Nina took the drawing and put it on top of the fridge.

"First we'll eat, and then we'll look," she said in a school-mistressy way.

60

A day passed, and with a fresh batch of files from the courier, Viktor sat at his typewriter. A spring sun was shining, and though it was still cold outside, in the kitchen its yellow rays not only flooded the table but even warmed the air. Work and the long-awaited warmth eased the burden of the recent past. And although all that had transpired was still, in a sense, present, the work of interspersing the philosophico-literary with facts underlined in red, provided an escape from affliction and all that served to remind him of his own helplessness.

One of his coffee breaks was enlivened by his suddenly calling to mind having written, some time ago, an *obelisk* on one Safronov. Who he had been and the nature of his attainments underlined in red Viktor had completely forgotten. But he felt sure that it was this Safronov whom he and Misha had buried a few days before. He couldn't, of course, be absolutely sure, but the fact that the funeral had been so patently obituary-worthy seemed to confirm the accuracy of his guess.

The thought that he who had first written the obituary had then attended the funeral, in the role of inspector to check that burial was indeed taking place, even brought a smile to his face.

Nina had taken Sonya to the Dnieper for a walk, so there was nothing to distract him from work. And that day work went smoothly. Reading through what he had written, he was well satisfied, and forged ahead with his improvisations on other people's deaths.

With four *obelisks* completed, he squinted out of the window at the sun, and went over to the stove. He put the kettle on and walked about the flat. Misha was standing by the balcony door, as if in expectation of an icy draught, and Viktor squatted down beside him.

"How are we doing?" he asked, taking a good look at him. "Very nicely, very nicely," he said, answering for his penguin and straightening up.

Noticing two framed drawings on the wall, he went over. One was the familiar portrait of Misha, the other – a threesome and a tiny penguin. *Uncle Vik, me, Nina and Misha* said the wobbly letters, but then, obviously in Nina's hand, *Uncle* had been corrected to *Daddy*, and *Nina* to *Mummy*. Nina's writing was neat and schoolmistressy. The signature at the bottom looked as if it had been improved by Teacher. All that was missing was the mark. Eight out of ten, probably, in view of the two corrections.

That drawing gave him a chilly feeling. He didn't care for Nina's corrections. There was a certain violence about them, to words and to the actual situation. The fact that the drawing was hung rather high up where Sonya could see it only by standing on a chair, meant that Nina had made the corrections for herself and for him.

Nina, too, seemed to be pretending they were a family, nursing, like him perhaps, the illusion of their being a single entity. Only it was an illusion shattered daily, lightly and unintentionally, by Sonya, the words *Daddy* and *Mummy* being either unknown to her, or ones she saw no reason to employ.

She was closer to reality: too young to invent a complicated world for herself, and too straightforward to suspect the thoughts and feelings of two grown-ups.

Would she not like a child of her own? he wondered uneasily, his thoughts returning to Nina. To call her Mummy to the end

165

of her days? There would be no difficulty about that . . .

But was *he*, he fell to thinking, anxious to be called *Daddy*? He had no objection in principle. He had money, work, everything. Even a young, attractive woman capable of motherhood. There was no love in it. Love wasn't the main thing, but something that came with time. Maybe one had only to move to the country and a spacious two-storey house with all conveniences, for it to light up like a candle.

He shook his head as if to rid it of so foolish a notion.

61

March brought warmth. Every morning, like a conscientious caretaker, the sun climbed into the sky and shone its brightest.

Viktor was getting through the latest batch of files, breaking off at intervals to make coffee and take his cup out onto the balcony. Misha joined him occasionally, seeming also to enjoy the sun.

Just another five minutes, and then it was back to the kitchen table, to hammer away at the typewriter.

His sunny mood accorded easily with the poetic gloom of his *obelisks*. Even a recent, second *funeral with penguin* had failed to unsettle him, although it had meant sitting through the wake of the unknown departed. But, strange as it seemed, even that proved not so very terrible. Of the good 200 or so mourners not one paid Viktor any special attention. Apart, of course, from Lyosha, sitting beside him. But he had soon become drunk, and pushing his plate aside, had fallen asleep, head on table cloth, or, more precisely, his table napkin.

There were no speeches. The well-dressed men seated at the two long tables exchanged business-like looks of sorrow, raising glasses of vodka to each other – a form of silent association Viktor had no difficulty in imitating, raising his glass, inclining his head, and looking with genuine grief at those sitting opposite. His sadness was unfeigned, but had nothing to do with the departed. It was just that the ambience of these wakes oppressed him, added to which the company at table was mainly male – Viktor did, looking around, notice some women, but no more than three or four, of mature years and marked by their conspicuous mourning as the original sources of grief.

At the end, he was put into one of the cars waiting outside the restaurant, together with three other men who did not introduce themselves, but simply asked where he lived and told the driver where to go. A night delivery service with a vengeance. Arriving home at about one, he encountered Misha in the corridor.

"Why aren't you asleep?" he asked, happily drunk. "Must get your sleep. What if we have got to shoot off to the cemetery again tomorrow?"

A week had now passed with Viktor hammering away at his typewriter and rejoicing in spring and sunshine. And life seemed easy and carefree, despite painful moments and less frequent scruples over his own part in an ugly business. But what, in an ugly world, was ugly? No more than a tiny part of an unknown evil existing generally, but not personally touching him and his little world. And not to be fully aware of his part in that ugly something was clearly a guarantee of the indestructibility of his world, and of its tranquillity.

Turning again to the window, he let the sun fall on his face. Maybe he really should buy a little dacha, sit in summer at a table in the garden, writing in the fresh air. With Sonya, who would like growing things, pottering in flower beds and vegetable plots, and Nina content . . .

He thought back to their New Year dacha, to Sergey, and how they had sat before the fire. How long ago that had been! How long, though not much time had passed since then!

62

On Sunday the sun continued to shine, and although in the morning there had been a thin haze of cloud, by eleven it had dispersed, revealing a sky of springtime blue.

After breakfast Viktor, Nina and Sonya set off for Kreshchatik Street, leaving Misha on the balcony with a bowl of lunch, and the door ajar so that he could, if he wished, go back inside.

He took them first to *Café Passazh*, where they sat on the terrace. For Sonya and Nina he ordered ice-cream, and coffee for himself.

Sonya having chosen to sit facing the sun, now screwed up her eyes, shielding them with the palm of her hand, playing peekaboo, watched by a smiling Nina.

Sipping his coffee, Viktor spotted an open newspaper kiosk, and saying he wouldn't be a minute, left the table.

Returning with *Capital News*, he quickly ran an eye over the headlines and finding, to his joy, neither menace nor a single obelisk, went calmly back to page one, taking another sip of coffee.

Remarkable that on so fine a spring day the news should seem so amazingly peaceful. No shooting, no scandals. Quite the reverse, as if the paper was commanding its readers to be happy with life, with headlines inspiring gladness and hope.

NEW SUPERMARKET OPENED

PROGRESS IN NEGOTIATIONS WITH RUSSIA

TO ITALY WITHOUT A VISA

"Would you like to go to Italy, Sonya?" he asked jokingly.

Licking the little plastic spoon, she shook her head.

"No – I want to go on a swing," she said.

Nina wiped the ice-cream from Sonya's mouth with a napkin.

As they walked through the park above the Dnieper, they came to a play area, sat Sonya on a swing and swung her, laughing, high above the ground.

"No more! No more!" she cried after a few minutes.

And again they walked through the park, Sonya between them, holding their hands.

"I was thinking, Nina," he said as they walked, "we could buy a dacha."

She smiled and became thoughtful.

"That'd be nice," she said a minute later, having evidently pictured the dacha she would like.

At lunch-time they went back to the flat and ate there.

Sonya joined Misha on the balcony. Nina and Viktor sat in front of the TV.

A Ukrainian version of *Cine-Travelogue Club* was on. A pretty blonde in a bright yellow bathing costume stood on the deck of a motor vessel, telling of exotic islands, then appeared on the beach of just such an island, exchanging smiles with sun-bronzed natives. Every so often captions ran across the bottom of the screen, with the telephone numbers of travel agents.

"Why were you asking Sonya about Italy?" she asked with sudden interest.

"They've done away with the visa requirement."

"Could we go one day?" she asked dreamily.

The pretty blonde was back again, now dressed more warmly in tight knitted skirt and dark-blue jacket.

For the past year, she announced, a Ukrainian scientific research station has been operating in the Antarctic. In an earlier programme we appealed for contributions towards sending our scientists a planeload of supplies. Many of you have responded, but unfortunately more is still needed than the amount so far received. I appeal to private entrepreneurs and others with funds – on you depends whether our scientists will be able to continue their work in the Antarctic. Have pencil and paper ready for the account number to which sponsor donations can be made, and a telephone number on which you can hear details of what your money will be spent on.

Darting to the kitchen, Viktor seized a pen and a sheet of paper, and returned in time to write down the numbers from the screen.

"What's that for?" Nina asked in surprise.

He shrugged. "Thought I might send them $20," he said uncertainly. "In memory of Pidpaly. I told you about him, remember? I've got a cutting about the station somewhere."

Nina shot him a look of disapproval.

"Waste of money," she said. "It'll only get stolen. Remember how they collected for a hospital for the Chernobyl children?"

Viktor said nothing, folded the paper and put it in his pocket. What business was it of hers where he sent his money?

63

Towards the end of March rain set in.

With the disappearance of the sun Viktor's spirits slumped. He worked away at his typewriter as before, but painfully slowly and with little inspiration. Even so, *obelisk* quality remained unimpaired, and reading over what he had written, he was invariably satisfied. No longer was his professionalism dependent on his mood.

Nina and Sonya kept to the flat for days on end.

Sometimes, when Nina went to the shops, Sonya, evidently weary of Misha's company, came into the kitchen to distract Viktor. With great forbearance he answered her questions, breathing a sigh of relief when he heard Nina return. Sonya then ran to her and he got back to work.

When Lyosha rang to say there was a funeral the next day, his spirits hit rock bottom. He spent ten minutes attempting to convey that it was too raw, too wet, that he was feeling low, as well as worried lest Misha catch a chill. Lyosha heard him out, then said that he, Viktor, was not all that essential. The animal was the main requirement. "You stay at home," he said finally, "I'll take Misha and bring him back afterwards. I'll keep an umbrella over him at the cemetery, so he doesn't catch cold."

A solution, a partial victory, Viktor decided, glad to give the funeral a miss.

And while he felt sorry for Misha there was nothing he could do about it. The possible consequences of a sudden refusal to release him for graveside attendance were all too obvious.

Viktor's firmness paid off handsomely. The next time Lyosha

did not expect him to participate. It was agreed that in future Lyosha would collect Misha and bring him back, and surprisingly this change of arrangement was not reflected in the amount of his honorarium. Each time it was the same $1,000, only now more easily come by, without any standing at gravesides or obligatory wakes. Misha was now earning on his own account, and the whole thing savoured of penguin hire.

Viktor was irked, of course, to think what Misha received for a single appearance, against his wage of $300. And though both lots of money came to him, the underlying inequality remained. There was nothing for it but to bow yet again to the inevitable. None of which in any way affected his attachment to Misha.

Ought he, he wondered, to ask the Chief for a rise, but immediately he sensed it wouldn't be worth the effort. He was, after all, fairly relaxed in his work. No one breathed down his neck or chased him for his *obelisks*. He was his own master. Batch completed, he rang up and swapped it with the courier for another. He had money enough, and so no cause for complaint.

No, all was as it should be, and God grant it stayed that way. And when the rainy spell was over, he could start looking for a dacha!

And as he visualized a little house surrounded by a garden, a hammock stretched between two sturdy trees, and himself kindling a fire for kebabs, his mood brightened.

All would be well, said the persuasive voice of his imagination, all beauty and bright sun.

And Viktor believed it.

But the rain and the task of *obelisk*-writing continued. And funerals involving Misha became more frequent, regardless of the rain, as if there had been a rise in the death-rate among those whose friends and relatives could not imagine a funeral without a penguin.

The day after one such funeral, as Viktor was studying a fresh batch of files, Sonya dashed in in great alarm.

"Uncle Vik, Misha's sneezing!"

Viktor went to the bedroom, and for the first time ever saw Misha lying on his side on his camel-hair blanket, trembling and wheezing.

Viktor stood paralysed with fear, at a loss what to do.

"Nina!" he shouted.

"She's at Sergey's mum's," said Sonya.

"Hold on, Misha, hold on," he said in a voice charged with emotion, gently stroking him. "We'll think of something."

Going to the living room, he turned, not very hopefully, to V in the telephone book, and to his amazement found no fewer than ten vets listed. But what experience would any of them have of treating penguins? Dogs and cats would be more in their line.

In spite of these doubts, he rang the first number.

"Is Nikolay Ivanovich there?" he asked the woman who answered, having checked he had got his names right.

"Hold on."

"Yes?" came a man's voice almost immediately.

"Sorry, but I've got a problem – my penguin's ill."

"*Penguin?*" the voice repeated, and Viktor knew at once that he had got the wrong man. "Not my province, but I can tell you who to ring."

"You can?" He sighed with relief. "I'll get a pen."

Viktor wrote the number – that of one David Yanovich – on the directory, and dialled without replacing the receiver.

"Well," said David Yanovich, when he had heard him out,

"if you've got that sort of animal, you'll have the money for treatment. Address?"

"Is the vet coming?" asked Sonya, as Viktor came back and sat down beside Misha on the floor.

"Yes."

"Like Dr Dolittle?" she asked sadly.

He nodded.

Half an hour later David Yanovich arrived: short, rather bald, with a frozen smile and kind eyes.

"Where's the patient then?" he asked, coming in and removing his shoes.

"In there." Viktor indicated the door. "Like some slippers?"

"No thanks." He quickly hung his mack on the hook, and briefcase in hand, made for the door, his socks leaving moist prints on the linoleum.

"Now then," he said, squatting down beside Misha.

He felt Misha all over, peered into his eyes, then, producing a stethoscope, sounded him front and back, like a normal doctor. Returning the stethoscope to his briefcase, he gazed at him deep in thought.

"Well?"

David Yanovich scratched the back of his neck, and sighed. "Hard to say, but clearly not good. It all depends, I'm afraid, on how you're placed financially. It's not my fee I'm talking about. There's not much I can do. He needs to go to a clinic."

"And what will that cost?" Viktor asked cautiously.

David Yanovich gestured helplessly. "It won't be cheap – that's for sure. If you take my advice, the Theophania Clinic's the place – $50 a day, but with the guarantee that they'll do everything possible. There's a hospital for scientists nearby, and their clinic rents time on their tomograph – an added guarantee of correct diagnosis. And quite a few good doctors from the hospital earn a bit on the side working at the clinic."

"Ordinary doctors?" Viktor asked in surprise.

David Yanovich shrugged. "Why not? You don't imagine animals are any different internally, do you? Their illnesses, yes. So I'll ring the Theophania from here if you like, and get a car sent."

"Please do."

Pocketing a mere $20 for attending, David Yanovich departed. An hour later another vet arrived who also examined Misha, sounding and feeling him all over.

"Right," he said, "we'll take him. And don't worry, you won't be conned. Three days diagnosis, and we'll know. If we can cure him, we will, if not . . ." He shruggged. "We'll bring him back, so as not to waste your money. Here," he handed Viktor a card. "Not mine, Ilya Semyonovich's – he'll be treating your pet."

The vet departed, leaving his card and taking Misha.

Sonya cried. The rain rained on. An unfinished *obelisk* protruded from the typewriter, but Viktor didn't feel like work. Legs against the hot radiator, he stood at the bedroom window, tears welling, as if in chain reaction to Sonya's, and through his tears, watched raindrops doing their best to cling to the glass. The wind set them quivering and away they shot finally, only to be replaced by fresh drops, and continue the senseless battle with the wind.

64

That night Viktor was unable to sleep. He could hear Sonya sobbing in the sitting room. The phosphorescent hands of the alarm clock showed that it was getting on for two. Only Nina was asleep, breathing heavily.

Naturally, she had been distressed at the news when she got back from Sergey's mother's. She had worn herself out vainly trying to comfort Sonya, and fallen asleep as soon as her head had touched the pillow.

Viktor felt strangely irritated that she should be sleeping peacefully. For an instant Nina seemed completely alien, utterly indifferent to him and Sonya, while Sonya seemed closer, and the two of them the more akin for their shared concern for Misha.

Looking at her, lying there with her back to him, he realized that it wasn't her sleeping peacefully that had caused his momentary irritation, but more his own peace-denying wakefulness.

Endeavouring not to wake her, he got up, put on his dressing-gown, went to the sitting room, and bent over Sonya.

She was sleeping, but uneasily, and still sobbing.

He stood for a minute or two, then went to the kitchen, shut the door behind him, and without switching on the light, went and sat down at the table.

The measured tick of the old alarm clock on the window ledge was amplified by the darkness and silence. It was surprisingly loud and he gazed, perplexed, at the tiny source of ticking lurking in the gloom. He wanted to silence it. He held it up to his eyes. The correct time, which it was the work of this simple, reliable mechanism to provide, did not interest him. Complete silence was all he wanted, but the tick grew even louder, and realizing that, stupid as it seemed, it was in fact time alone that was capable of stopping the clock, Viktor took it into the corridor, deposited it by the main door, and came back.

After listening hard and failing to detect so much as a distant tick, he felt reassured.

In the one lighted window of the block opposite, there was a woman.

She was sitting at a table reading. And although it wasn't possible to see her face, he felt a sudden warmth and sympathy towards her, as to a companion in misfortune.

He watched her sitting motionless, chin propped on hands, only occasionally lowering her right hand to turn a page.

For a moment it seemed brighter outside. A pale yellow half moon had emerged. But having revealed itself to Viktor, it hid again in unseen cloud.

He looked back at the lighted window. The woman was at the stove. She lit the burner, put the kettle on, then returned to the table and her book.

It was good that the rain had stopped, he thought, remembering the quivering drops on the window pane.

Turning to the closed door, he remembered Misha's habit of pushing it open, standing there, then coming over as he sat at the table and snuggling against his knee. If only it would open now, and Misha be standing there!

After sitting for half an hour or so, he stole back to the bedroom, and slipped under the blanket. With Sonya's sobbing still in his ears, he fell asleep.

Next morning Nina woke him.

"Someone came in the night again," she said, plainly worried.

"Brought something again, have they?" he asked sleepily.

She shook her head. "No, but they've left an alarm clock inside the door."

"That was me," he muttered in an effort to reassure her.

"Whatever for?" she asked in surprise.

"Because of its ticking," he said, dozing off again, oblivious to her bewilderment and questioning looks.

He woke at about 11.00. The flat was quiet. The sun was shining.

In the kitchen he found his breakfast and a note:

Back soon. We've gone for a walk. Nina.

After he had washed, he picked up the card left by the vet and rang the clinic.

"Can I speak to Ilya Semyonovich?"

"That's me," said a velvety voice.

"I'm the owner of the penguin . . . Misha."

"Greetings," said the invisible Ilya Semyonovich. "Well, how can I put it? Provisionally, it's flu, with serious complications. We're doing a tomograph this evening, and then we can be more precise."

"How is he at the moment?"

"No change, I'm afraid."

"Can I visit?"

"I'm afraid not. You must be patient. Ring daily and I'll update you," Ilya Semyonovich promised.

Returning to the kitchen, Viktor ate two boiled eggs, drank tea, and got out the typewriter from under the table. Sticking out of it was an unfinished obelisk on a certain Bondarenko, Director of Broadway Private Funeral Services. He smiled at the bitter irony of it. He could imagine how *professional* his funeral would be, with colleagues standing decorously beside a splendid, gilt-handled coffin.

What did *he* have underlined? he wondered, no longer able to remember anything from Bondarenko's file.

He found the three pages and looked.

In 1995, at Belogorodok, in a common grave in the village cemetery, Vyacheslav Bondarenko interred a number of mutilated, unidentified corpses. There are grounds for supposing that among the interred were the bodies of Captain Golovatko of the Anti Organized Crime Department, and Major Prochenko of the Ukrainian Security Service. Bondarenko is supected of involvement in a number of similar interments in villages in the Kiev region over the period 1992–94.

With no sense of bitter irony, Viktor got up, made coffee, and went out onto the balcony.

To take his mind off funerals for five minutes, he looked at the windows of the block opposite, trying to determine which had been the one with the light on. But now in broad daylight they all looked the same.

65

The next morning also began with a call to the Theophania Clinic. But Ilya Semyonovich wasn't there, and Viktor had nothing to tell Sonya who was standing beside him.

"I'll try again in half an hour," he promised.

Without a word, she went over to the balcony door.

"How about going to the circus this evening?" Nina asked, bending down to her.

Sonya shook her head.

As Viktor was on his way to start work in the kitchen, the phone rang. Sonya and Nina stood and listened. He lifted the receiver, also expecting it to be the veterinary clinic, but it was the Chief, and he was evidently displeased.

"Philosophical masterpieces are not what I want," he declared, almost shouting. "Just do a simple professional job, and kindly be quick about it. I can't wait a whole week for just five or six texts."

Viktor nodded gloomily as he listened.

"Are you with me?" demanded the Chief in a calmer voice, as if wearied by his outburst.

"Yes," replied Viktor replacing the receiver. He had grown used to phone conversations with the Chief being too business-like to include *hellos* or *goodbyes*.

"Who was that?" asked Nina from the balcony door.

"Work," he sighed, returning the receiver to his ear.

He dialled the number of the veterinary clinic.

This time Ilya Semyonovich was there. "We need to meet," he said.

Viktor detected a note of doom in his voice. "Shall I come out to the clinic?"

"No point. We'll meet in town. *Old Kiev*, Kreshchatik Street, at eleven."

"How shall I recognize you?" asked Viktor.

"I don't think there'll be many there. Still, grey mack, tweed cap, thin, shortish, moustache . . ."

"What do they say?" Sonya asked impatiently.

"He's getting on," he lied. "I'm going to see the vet and find out exactly."

He was filled with foreboding. Otherwise why this meeting at a café in Kreshchatik Street? For good news there was always the phone. Maybe the vet wanted to talk money. Viktor had, after all, paid nothing so far, and it was $50 a day for Misha's stay in the clinic alone.

The thought that money might be the subject of their conversation in the café reassured him a little.

The sun was shining. By the entrance, two girls were jumping over stretched elastic, and he gave them a wide berth.

Down in the basement café Ilya Semyonovich was waiting, standing at a tall table on which was a cup of coffee. No one else was in evidence, not even behind the counter or at the coffee machine.

Ilya Semyonovich greeted him, and went and banged loudly on the counter.

"Another coffee," he told the woman who appeared from behind the scenes, then came back.

"So what's the score?" asked Viktor.

"He appears to have a congenital heart defect," said the vet. "Radical treatment for the influenza could kill him . . . But even without the influenza, his chances are virtually nil. Unless . . ." He looked expectantly at Viktor.

"Is it a question of money?"

"It is. But money apart, there's still a question of principle, pure and simple, which is for you to decide. I have no idea just how much your penguin means to you."

"One coffee!" shouted the counter woman addressing Viktor's back.

By the time he fetched it, she had disappeared.

"Just tell me how much," Viktor said, coming back to the tall table.

"All right. I'll put it as simply as I can." He took a deep breath. "Misha's only chance is a heart operation, or, to be more precise, a transplant."

"But how?" Viktor looked at him in despair. "Where do you get another penguin heart?"

"That," said Ilya Semyonovich, "is where the question of principle arises. I've consulted the professor of cardiology at the hospital for scientists . . . In our opinion the heart of a three- or four-year-old child would serve."

Viktor choked on his coffee, and spilt some as he put down his cup.

"Given a successful outcome, that could give him several more years of life at least. Otherwise . . ." He gestured vaguely. "But to cover your points: the actual operation would cost a total of $15,000. Which isn't too bad. As to a donor heart . . . You could try your channels over that, or we could try for you. I can't, at the moment, actually give a price for that. Organs have been known to turn up absolutely gratis."

"*Try my channels?* How do you mean?" he asked, dumbfounded.

"I mean that there are children's hospitals in Kiev, each with its life-support unit," Ilya Semyonovich said calmly. "You can get to know the doctors, not telling them the organ's for a penguin. Just say you've a transplant need for the heart of a three-to-four-year-old. Offer good recompense. They'll keep you informed."

Viktor shook his head. "No."

"Why not?" asked Ilya Semyonovich. "All right. You need to think it over quietly. You've got my number. The only thing is,

182

don't be too long. It's your money-meter that's ticking. I'll await your call, then."

Ilya Semyonovich went, leaving Viktor alone.

Disinclined to finish his cold coffee, Viktor left too, and set off along Kreshchatik Street in the direction of the main post office.

The sun was shining, but he didn't notice. People were passing, but he paid no attention. Jostled by some young fellow in the underpass, he didn't so much as look back, and himself bumped into a gypsy woman trying to beg money from him.

Something was wrong with this life, he thought, walking with downcast eyes. Or life itself had changed, and was as it used to be – simple, comprehensible – only on the outside. Inside, it was as if the mechanism was broken, and now there was no knowing what to expect of a familiar object – be it a loaf of Ukrainian bread or a street pay telephone. Beneath every surface, inside every tree, every person, lurked an invisible alien something. The seeming reality of everything was only a relic of childhood.

Just beyond the former Lenin Museum, he stopped and gazed around rather oddly, as if seeking out hitherto unnoticed details of the familiar cityscape. He considered, beyond the park steps, the steel arch of the Two Nations Friendship Monument, the ruins of the Philharmonic Hall, a hoarding graphically awash with French shampoo: *Your Hair – The Envy of All!*

A 62 bus full of people drew up below the hoarding. Several people alighted, then it drove straight on, leaving an angry crowd behind at the stop, and turned right down Vladimir Rise.

He watched, then he too set off down the hill to Podol, passing the lower funicular station and the main river terminal. Vladimir Rise levelled off and ran into Pyotr Sagaydachny Street.

He paused outside the *Bacchus Bar*, and went in.

He ordered a glass of dry red and sat at a table. Sipping his wine, he sighed. Why did it have to be a child's heart? Why not a dog's? Or a sheep's?

At a neighbouring table a group of young men were lacing their beer with vodka.

Viktor drank more wine, relishing its astringency. Agitated, nervous thoughts gave way to calm.

A penguin did, after all, have much more in common with Man than with a dog or a sheep – penguin and Man both being erect creatures, bipeds, not quadrupeds . . . And unlike Man, the penguin seemed never to have had quadruped ancestors.

And he remembered Pidpaly's manuscript – the only thing he had ever read on penguins – remembered that it was the father penguins who reared and brought up their young, remaining faithful husbands year in, year out; that penguins were adept at orientating themselves by the sun; that they had an innate sense of community. He remembered Pidpaly's flat, the smell of smoke . . . And his thoughts returned to Misha.

He finished the wine and ordered another. The group of young men went, walking unsteadily. Viktor was left alone. He looked at the clock: 12.30. The sun peeped into the bar, silhouetting his glass on the table and providing the scattered crumbs with tiny shadows.

Misha must have the operation, he decided, emboldened by the wine. Let them do it all. There should be enough money. He could take some from the bag on top of the wardrobe. The fact that it was Sonya's didn't matter.

Back at the flat, Viktor went without lunch and lay down for a nap. Nina and Sonya were out.

Waking towards four with a muzzy head, he made coffee and sat down at the table.

When his muzziness eased, and the coffee's warmth had restored him just a little, his thoughts returned to Misha. But self-assurance had gone from him with the effects of the wine. Dragging his typewriter out from under the table, he tried to lose himself in work. He thought back to the Chief's phone call. The Chief was right. He must turn over a new leaf. And frozen into immobility, he sat at the typewriter before a white sheet of paper anxious to be typed on.

He picked up the folder and looked through the files. There was just one he hadn't dealt with. He began to read.

Nina and Sonya returned a little later.

"We've been at Sergey's mother's," Nina said, helping Sonya out of her coat. "She's worried. He hasn't phoned for two weeks . . ."

"How's Misha?" Sonya asked, coming into the kitchen in her socks.

"Go and put your slippers on," said Viktor sternly. "The vet's promised to cure him," he called after her as she went obediently to retrieve them from the corridor. "But he'll have to stay in hospital."

"Can we go and see him?"

"No," he said, "they don't let people in."

66

A day passed, but Viktor had still not rung the Theophania Clinic. He had completed his last *obelisk*, and was now awaiting the Chief's courier.

Nina and Sonya had gone for a walk somewhere, and taking

advantage of their absence, he counted Sonya's dollars. Just over $40,000. He refastened the fat wad with elastic bands and put it back. Then he counted his own money, the bulk of it earned by Misha. Almost $10,000.

"I must phone," he told himself, and at that moment the doorbell rang.

It was the taciturn courier, a man of pensionable age in an old drape overcoat, who took the folder, put it in his briefcase, produced another, nodded and hurried off down the stairs.

Viktor watched him go and went back into the flat, throwing the folder on the kitchen table. He went to the phone in the living room and again he dithered. Something was holding him back.

"I must phone," he kept telling himself, still rooted to the spot, just looking at the instrument as if it could ring on its own and say what was necessary.

At last he did dial the number of the clinic. He asked for Ilya Semyonovich, and learning that he was out, felt amazingly relieved.

He did not ring any more that day, but got down to work, and by the time Nina and Sonya returned had written three *obelisks*. Another two and he could ring the Chief – show him how fast he was working!

Next morning Lyosha rang.

"Very big funeral tomorrow, old chap."

"It'll have to do without him, I'm afraid," Viktor said wearily. "He caught a chill at the last one, and it's not certain at the moment whether he'll pull through."

He gave the horrified Lyosha a full account.

"Listen," said Lyosha, "if I'm to blame, let me sort it out. Where is he?"

Viktor gave him Ilya Semyonovich's number.

"Good. I'll get back to you," he said. "Don't go grieving."

That evening he rang back.

"It's going to be all right," he said reassuringly. "The boys are taking on the financial side and everything to do with the operation. He's a good fellow, your Ilya Semyonovich. He'll ring each day, and keep you informed . . . By the bye," he asked out of the blue, "could *you* come with me tomorrow? Taking the wake in after?"

"So it's me who's the penguin," Viktor said gloomily.

Back at his typewriter he felt suddenly both hopeful and distinctly alarmed. The *boys* – and he could guess the sort – had decided to pay for the operation, and were, on the face of it, looking out for a donor heart . . .

The present situation had the feel of a horror film about it, and Viktor didn't like horror films.

He shook his head to dispel the association, and returned to *the boys.* Why should they decide to take it on? Were they that good-natured? That fond of animals? Indebted to him in some way? Or to Misha?

Quickly wearying of questions, he determined to think of something else, but still his thoughts revolved around the sick penguin.

He suddenly remembered the television programme and the pretty presenter appealing for people to sponsor a plane with provisions to be sent to the Ukrainian research station in the Antarctic. He looked for the piece of paper he had noted the account and telephone numbers on.

A sudden happy thought struck him. If Misha survived, he must be sent home to the Antarctic on that plane. Viktor would offer to contribute on condition that they released his penguin amid the icy wastes . . . Make an offer they couldn't refuse.

Cheered by the idea, he tackled the remaining obelisks with enthusiasm, and two hours later had finished them.

That evening Ilya Semyonovich rang.

"You know it's all OK?" he said.

"Yes."

"I must say, you've got good friends. Your Misha's stable at the moment. We're preparing for the operation."

"Have you got all you need?"

"Not yet. A matter of two or three days, I think. I'll ring tomorrow."

Half an hour later, after her supper, Sonya asked how Misha was.

"On the mend," he said with relief.

67

Viktor delayed going to bed. Sonya and Nina must long since have been in the land of dreams, but he was still in the kitchen in the dark, watching the lights go out one after another in the opposite block.

He didn't feel like sleep. It was not a case of insomnia. He was simply enjoying the silence and peace of watching the city fall asleep. And he was no longer irritated by the ticking of the alarm clock, now back on the window ledge. His agitation was past. His thoughts, too, under the influence of this peace, had stopped racing, and were now flowing with the ease of an unhurried river.

After all these shocks, unpleasant discoveries and the dark suspicions they prompted, and moments better forgotten than understood and accepted as commonplace, his life seemed to be resuming its normal course. And normality was the only state from which to contemplate the future – a future to be achieved only by striving forward, without stopping to throw light on some mystery or going into any change in the nature of life itself. Life was a road, and if departed from at a tangent, the longer for it. And a long road was a long life – a case where to travel was better than to arrive, the point of arrival being, after all, always the same: death.

And off at a tangent he had gone, feeling his way past closed doors, but leaving behind him what traces of his contact they retained. All the same, they did stay with him, those traces of contact – in his memory, in a no longer burdensome past.

In the block opposite, only three lighted windows, and the one he sought not among them. Whoever was pottering behind those was of no interest. He wanted to see the woman he had watched during his last sleepless night. But even her absence failed to disrupt his peace.

He had, it seemed, divined the secret of longevity. Longevity depended on peace. Peace was the source of self-assurance, and self-assurance allowed one to cleanse one's life of needless upsets, twists and turns. Self-assurance allowed one to take decisions for the prolonging of one's life. Self-assurance led to the future.

He looked into that future and saw so clearly, as if for the first time in his life, everything that obstructed the peaceful path for him. It was, oddly enough, all connected indirectly with his beloved Misha. And although Misha himself had nothing to do with it, he had become an involuntary cause of complication in Viktor's life. Misha had drawn him into a mournful circle of people with an enhanced degree of mortality, and now Misha alone could free him from them. With Misha out of the picture, Lyosha and his binoculars would be also, as well as gilt-handled coffins. Of the two evils in Viktor's life, only one would remain – his work. But that was an evil he had long reconciled himself to – someone else's evil, to which, at the rate of $300 a month, Viktor imparted a philosophical dimension. It was an evil to which he was an indirect rather than a main contributor.

It was pleasing to picture Misha against a backdrop of Antarctic wastes. It was the only solution – to the advantage of them both. Freedom. Provided the operation went well. And even if the boys now shouldering the costs were to take exception to the disappearance of their penguin, what could they do? He was, after all, blessed with that mysterious protection, spoken of in awe by the late Misha-non-penguin and his enemy-friend Sergey Chekalin.

Seeming to discern the calm, measured rhythm of his future life, he smiled contentedly.

In the block opposite, the last window went dark, and the diffuse light of the moon was all the brighter.

68

Several spring days passed. Every evening the telephone rang and Ilya Semyonovich reported on Misha's condition, which was, like Viktor's – and that of the weather – stable. Nina and Sonya disappeared early each morning, Nina having conceived the idea of showing Sonya spring. They were studying it like a school subject. It was a game they both seemed to enjoy and Viktor enjoyed their absence for he was able to work in peace. *Obelisks* flowed fast and free, and he expected a call and words of praise from the Chief. But the Chief did not call. Nor, apart from Ilya Semyonovich, did anyone else. District Militiaman Sergey, now far away, had been the only one to make calls that did not tie Viktor down to something. Who else was there lurking on the shady side of his life? Lyosha, bodyguard of *big-affair* funerals? He would ring eventually. No doubt about that. And he wasn't so bad, either. Lyosha, too, was living at a tangent, having found his niche and occupied it. No mean achievement, perhaps, nowadays. And having done so, the thing was not to excite envy – lest, God forbid, someone thought the niche too good for you . . .

At about 3.00 Ilya Semyonovich rang.

"We operated last night," he said. "All's fine at the moment. No sign of the organ being rejected."

Viktor was delighted, thanked him, and asked when he would be able to bring Misha home.

"Not for a while, I think," said Ilya Semyonovich. "Six weeks is the rehabilitation period . . . But I'll keep you informed. It could be shorter. We'll see."

Viktor made coffee and went out onto the balcony, screwing up his eyes against the sun. An amazingly cool, gentle breeze was blowing. There was a pleasant feeling of freshness, and the early warmth of a still unsteady infant sun. An amazing feeling. The fragility of a light breeze and the continuity of the sun in combination. Warmth and freshness. That was what woke life, called life to the surface of the Earth.

The coffee was weak, but he didn't want it strong. Strong coffee seemed now to savour of winter, of having to struggle with lethargy, too little daylight, and a weary expectation of warmth.

He could now ring the Antarctic Committee. And he, lover of warmth, would be happy here, and Misha would be happy there.

Returning to the living room he paused for a minute by Sonya's framed family portrait with penguin.

He smiled and sighed, feeling a certain sense of pride in himself and his solution, and thought how much easier it was to decide someone else's fate than one's own. Particularly as all attempts at changing his own had only led to further undesirable, more burdensome consequences. All change, as it turned out, was for the worse, regardless of its nature.

69

The offices of the Antarctic Committee were in two adjoining rooms behind a door bearing the nostalgic legend Party Office, on the second floor of the admin building of an aircraft factory.

He arrived at about eleven, having rung in advance. To have mentioned his penguin over the phone would have been foolish – leading them to think he was either having them on or cracked. He had therefore presented himself as a potential sponsor.

At the factory gate he had a five-minute wait until a lean, grey-suited man of about 45 came down to collect him. This was Valentin Ivanovich, Chairman of the Antarctic Committee, who was, as befitted a raiser of funds, courteous and welcoming. Having first provided coffee, he opened the door to the adjoining office.

"You see, it's mostly provisions we get offered," he said, indicating rows of cardboard boxes and a corner filled with tins. "We take everything, even if the sell-by date's long expired. It's good to have the offer. Sometimes we're given money. The Southern Construction Bank has donated $300. Money's what we prefer, of course. We need fuel for the plane. We have pilots to pay for sitting idle."

Viktor nodded sympathetically.

Returning to the first office, Valentin Ivanovich got out some documents detailing the provisions and the amount of cash collected.

Viktor leafed through them, noticing that one sponsor had donated an enormous quantity of Chinese tinned stew.

"That's not all our stuff in there," Valentin Ivanovich added. "We store equipment and warm clothing separately. And we also have two drums of sunflower oil."

"When do you fly?" Viktor asked.

"Ninth of May, Victory Day as was. We're making intermediate landings, so we've had to give advance notice. But how, if I may ask, would you like to assist? Cash or provisions?"

"Cash," replied Viktor. "Subject to one condition."

"Go ahead," Valentin Ivanovich invited, staring hard.

"A year ago, when the zoo had no food for its animals, I adopted a penguin. And now I'd like to send him to the Antarctic, to his natural environment . . . That's really what I want."

For just an instant the bright blue eyes of the Chairman betrayed a flash of irony, but his face remained as grave as Viktor's own. They stared as if playing *who-looks-away-first*, but after a minute or two the Chairman lowered his thoughtful gaze to the table.

"And how much will you donate for this passenger?" he asked, without looking up.

"A couple of thousand dollars."

Viktor had no wish to haggle. So far all had gone well, the quizzical look – whether of irony or mistrust – having in no way influenced the business in hand.

For a minute or so Valentin Ivanovich pondered in silence.

"In cash?" he asked, looking keenly at him.

Viktor nodded.

"Good," said the Chairman, "we'll take your passenger. Could you produce the money in the next day or two, and the penguin at about nine on the day of departure? Take-off is at about midday."

Viktor's mood as he walked home along the sunny street was curiously one of anxiety. The ease with which he had decided Misha's fate set him thinking about his own. On the 9th of May he would be left alone. And although he would have Nina and Sonya at his side, their autonomous, apparently independent presence, wouldn't make him forget Misha.

Affection was not something he expected from Nina and Sonya, not being affectionate towards them himself. Was it then simply a protracted *we're-a-family* game? Maybe. But it appeared to suit Nina. Little Sonya didn't understand, of course. The presence of grown-ups was a natural feature of her life. Of her own parents she seemed to have no recollection at all. Perhaps he should try to grow fond of Nina and Sonya, get them to respond, so that their strange union became that of a genuine family.

70

April was drawing to a close. The city, made verdant by warmth, was preparing for the chestnut trees to blossom. But the pace of Viktor's life had been reduced. The last time the courier collected the finished *obelisks* he had left nothing in exchange. Viktor rang the Chief, and the Chief said that there would be no work for the time being. Viktor was caught unawares by this sudden hiatus. He had been wrong-footed. Thus far, all had gone according to plan: he had long since delivered the $2,000 to Valentin Ivanovich, and Ilya Semyonovich was reporting daily on the progress of Misha's convalescence. Now suddenly, this.

Nina had returned to the subject of buying a dacha, and was bringing home the weekly advertisers. He patiently studied everything she marked. It seemed to him they ought to get moving and buy their little house with garden as quickly as possible, so as to have it right for the three of them in the summer. But at the same time he fell victim to a certain passivity.

After the 9th of May it would all be over he thought, connecting his strange state with lack of work and anticipation of Misha's departure.

Sonya asked after Misha less and less often, and that pleased him. He was by now almost convinced that the disappearance of the penguin from her life would be achieved with a minimum of fuss. He was more fearful and sorry for himself, having no difficulty in imagining the occasions when he would soon miss his Misha.

But the decision having been taken, and therefore out of his hands, he was spared any premature self-pity.

Lyosha rang.

"First-rate, the whole thing!" he said. "In a couple of weeks we'll be drinking your penguin's health at someone's wake!"

Yes, thought Viktor, and for the first time in ages he managed a smile.

Nina came back from a visit to Sergey's mother with a post-office chit for a parcel.

They sat down to supper. It was early evening, getting on for six.

"Funny," Nina said. "it looks as if it's from Sergey, but it's not his writing. And there's $20 at exchange rate to pay. As if it's from abroad."

"We *are* abroad," said Viktor gloomily, applying a blunt knife to his chop.

"Mine's tough," complained Sonya.

"I'll cut it up for you," said Viktor, leaning over and sawing away.

"The knives need sharpening," said Nina.

"I'll see to it," he promised.

"Will you come when I go to the post office?" Nina asked later as they drank tea. "In case it's heavy."

"Of course."

That evening Sonya again fell asleep in front of the television.

They put her on the settee, covered her with a blanket and turned down the volume. They watched the latest Mel Gibson block-buster to its bloody conclusion, before finally retiring to bed.

Next morning, having paid $20 at the rate of exchange, they received the parcel: a fairly heavy cardboard box with a diagonal FRAGILE – HANDLE WITH CARE strip.

"That's not his writing!" Nina declared, seeing the address on the cardboard box.

As Viktor picked up the parcel, there was a chinking sound inside.

Taking another look at the warning strip, he shook his head. "Sounds as if something's broken," he said.

"$20 for nothing then," said Nina, far from pleased. "So we'll take it home first, and have a look. No sense in taking it straight to her. She'll only be upset if it's broken."

Back at the flat, they praised Sonya's latest drawings, then unpacked the box on the kitchen table and took out a strange, dark-green, four-sided vase with a little lid, wrapped round with sticky tape.

Was it copper? Viktor wondered, examining it.

"It's got something inside," Nina said. "And look! There's a letter."

It was a sheet of paper folded in two.

He watched while she read, stony-faced, lips moving, hands trembling. Saying nothing, she passed the letter to him.

Dear Sergey's Mother,

Militia Department, Krasnopresnensk, have asked me to write this on their behalf. Very likely because I, too, came here from Ukraine, from Donyetsk. And also because

197

Sergey and I were friends. He was a wonderful chap. I don't know what else to say. He died in the execution of his duty. It wasn't in Moscow it happened. He didn't want to go, but orders are orders. City MVD Finance gave us a problem: they would either pay just for burial – but way out beyond Orekhovo-Zuyevo – or pay for cremation. We from Ukraine thought cremation, as then he could still be buried at home. Please accept our condolences.

Nikolay Prokhorenko,
p.p. Militia Department, Krasnopresnensk.

Having read this, Viktor looked again at the four-sided urn. Nina slipped out into the corridor. He could hear her crying.

Gingerly he picked the urn up with both hands and gave it a gentle shake. A strange, dull, sand-like sound resulted. He put it back on the table.

As rattles went, one of the sadder sort, he thought gloomily. All that was left of Sergey.

From the bathroom came the sound of running water. A minute later Nina returned, wet-faced and red-eyed.

"I shan't tell his mother," she said. "It would kill her. We'll bury him ourselves."

Viktor nodded.

71

Several days passed. Time, continuing its snail-like pace, weighed heavily on him, and despite the warm sunny weather, he stayed indoors. A couple of times he dragged out his typewriter from under the table and tried to write, but thought and imagination seemed paralysed by the sight of the white paper.

He ought perhaps to have been reading – the popular crime report sections of the newspapers – in search of material and notables.

He remembered how he had winkled out the subjects of his first *obelisks* and wondered where they were now, those notables.

Standing on the window ledge where he had moved it to clear the table for lunch on the day they had received the parcel, was the dark-green four-sided urn. Whenever it caught his eye it made him think of Sergey, of New Year at his dacha, and of their winter picnics on the ice with Misha. And he felt a strange sense of happiness lost forever. Looking at the curious urn with its artificial dark-green patina, he could not believe that that was the new shell of Sergey's mortal remains. That, for him, was still simply a curiosity, a mute newcomer from another world. And its presence in the kitchen, while puzzling, roused no feeling of protest. It seemed alive, the velvety green of the patina, and the urn itself an animate object, in spite of its contents. And he could not believe it had anything to do with Sergey, his life or his death. No. If Sergey was no more, he *was no more*. In that urn or anywhere.

Towards evening Nina and Sonya returned.

"We had an uncle asking about you," said Sonya, busy

changing her shoes as Viktor looked out into the corridor.

"What uncle?" he asked, surprised.

"A young fat one," said Sonya.

His look of surprise was switched to Nina.

"Some friend of yours," she explained. "Just interested to know how you were at present, and what you were doing."

"He bought us an ice-cream," Sonya added.

For supper Nina roasted a chicken. And then, as they drank tea, produced a page of advertisements from her bag.

"Look," she passed it to Viktor, "seems ideal: Koncha-Zaspa, tenth of a hectare, and not expensive."

Two-storey dacha, he read, *four rooms, tenth hectare, new garden, $12,000.*

"Yes," he said, "we must ring."

Only immediately after, Ilya Semyonovich rang, and the dacha was forgotten.

"He's mobilizing, walking round the ward," said the vet.

"Can I fetch him?"

"Well, I think we should keep an eye on him for the next ten days."

"Would the 7th or 8th of May be all right for fetching him?"

"Yes, I think so."

With a sigh of relief Viktor replaced the receiver. Glancing towards the balcony he saw it was still light.

"Just going out for ten minutes for a stroll," he called from the corridor, putting on his trainers.

72

Two more days passed, bringing what was once Victory Day closer.

He did after all ring about the dacha in Koncha-Zaspa, and arranged to view it the coming Sunday. Nina felt sure it would be to their liking.

In this sort of weather any dacha would seem like paradise, he thought, standing on the balcony with his cup of coffee.

By midday the sun was scorching. There was a slight breeze, but even that was warm, like the wafting of a giant hair-drier.

After the ninth he would ring the Chief and get some work, he decided, otherwise he would be bored ... Or maybe they would break loose, the three of them, go to the Crimea for a fortnight. But then what about the dacha? No, they must see to that first. And if they bought it, why go to the Crimea?

Nina and Sonya came back at about five.

"What have you been doing?" he asked.

"We've been to Hydropark," said Nina, "boating."

"And people are swimming already," added Sonya.

"We saw your friend again," Nina said. "He's a bit odd."

"What friend?"

"The one who treated us to an ice-cream and asked about you."

Viktor thought for a moment.

"What does he look like?"

"Fattish, about 30." She shrugged. "Nothing special ... Sat at our table in the café outside the Metro."

"He asked did you love me," said Sonya. "And I told him you didn't much."

Viktor felt a growing sense of unease. Even among his former acquaintances there was no one fat and 30-ish.

"What else did he ask?"

Nina thought, looking at the ground.

"Oh – about your work. Whether or not you liked it . . . And if you were still writing stories . . . Used to enjoy them, he said. Oh, and could I show him something you'd written . . . Without your knowing . . . Writers were never keen on giving manuscripts to be read, he said."

"And what," he asked coldly, "did you say?"

"She said she'd have a look," said Sonya in her stead.

"I didn't," said Nina. "He said Kiev was a small place, and we'd meet again. I said nothing about manuscripts."

Who could it be, wondered Viktor. And why was he asking about him?

Finding no answer, he shrugged, went out onto the balcony, and leaning on the rail, looked down into the courtyard. The rectangle of asphalt was full of washing hung on lines stretched between white ferro-concrete posts. Children were playing nearby. On the left stood a white-painted skip at the base of which lay some old tin drums. Beyond, but not visible from the balcony, was the wasteland with the three dovecotes, where he, Misha and Sonya had sometimes walked in winter: *Plan View in Spring of Familiar Scene* . . .

He harked back in thought to the nosy, fat young man.

Maybe he was shadowing them, he thought, looking down into the courtyard again. How else could he know they were a family?

A couple of old men sat on the seat by the entrance, and by the next entrance people were also sitting. A number of youths were walking past the block opposite, quarrelling loudly.

Nothing and no one suspicious.

Reassured, he went back in.

73

That night sleep eluded him. Listening in the dark to Nina's calm breathing, and conscious of her warmth beside him, he fell to wondering who this pryer into his life might be, where he came from and he was after. And the curious question about loving Sonya.

Such thoughts were accompanied by a growing sense of alarm that rendered peace of mind and sleep ever more remote.

They *were* being tailed. And he must be too. So he would just go out less often.

Trying not to wake Nina, he eased himself out of bed, slipped on his dressing-gown, and went out onto the balcony.

The star-scattered heavens shed a pleasant freshness. The tense silence of the dormant city was oppressive. The windows opposite were all dark. And below, inactive for the night, the courtyard was a set without actors.

Still, if someone really was tailing them, they would be in a car, parked without lights at the entrance to the neighbouring block.

Leaning over the rail, he looked the length of the block, and seeing the entrance approach blocked by two parked vehicles, smiled ruefully at coming so close to persecution mania.

He returned to the bedroom, but not until first light did he fall asleep.

Next morning, restored by strong coffee to a state of cheerful irritability, he took a bath and shaved.

After breakfast Nina and Sonya got ready to go into town.

"Where today?" he asked Nina.

"Hydropark again. It's nice. They've got the amusements working."

As soon as they had left the flat he scanned the courtyard, face pressed to the kitchen window, then looked directly down to watch the entrance. When Nina and Sonya emerged, he scanned the courtyard again, and saw a short, solidly built man rise from a seat outside the opposite block, and follow slowly in the direction of the bus stop. After 20 metres or so he stopped and looked back. A *Moskvich* estate drew up. He got in beside the driver, and the car drove off.

Puzzled by what he had seen, Viktor quickly put on his shoes and left the flat.

The bus stop was deserted, the bus having left. He hitched a lift, and five minutes later was making his way down the Metro escalator.

The more he thought about this strange tailing and prying, the more puzzled he became. And that chap in the baggy football shirt and a car no heavy would be seen dead in – they somehow didn't tie up with his alarm and sense of danger at Nina's second mention of the nosy, fat young man.

Still, strange as it might appear, someone definitely was tailing Nina for the purpose of staging another chance meeting in town and asking more questions about him. Someone was onto him, and his only comfort was that close-cropped young men in tracksuits and the latest flashy imported cars had no part in this mystery.

That being so, he had nothing to fear. But the mystery remained, and had to be solved.

It occurred to him, sitting in the Metro train, that he was enjoying this game – or more precisely, this chance to clear things up for himself. His confidence had come back – as though he had once again been reminded of the *protection* he enjoyed, although he had never understood why. But given Misha-non-penguin and Sergey Chekalin's reverential mention of it at some point, it must be there, protecting him from something.

Bearing right as he left the Metro station, he stopped at a stand displaying dozens of sunglasses. Seated to the left of it, on a collapsible chair, was a girl of about 20, also in dark glasses.

Without stopping to think, he tried the rather old-fashioned drop-shapes, followed by some *Made-in-Taiwans*. When at last he had made his choice, he paid and put them on.

A smell of kebabs was in the air. Although it was a working day, the market area of Hydropark was fairly crowded. Most of the pavement tables were taken by people at a loose end. Finding one that was free, he ordered coffee and cognac, and still wearing his dark glasses, looked around.

No sign of Nina and Sonya, but against that he spotted another familiar face, a man of about 40 he had seen at several big funerals. He was sitting at a table outside the adjacent café with a tall elegant woman in a rather short belted blue frock. They were both drinking beer and chatting quietly.

Viktor watched for a few minutes, then took another look around.

The waitress brought his coffee and cognac and asked to be paid. When she had gone, he sipped his cognac and coffee, and forgot about Sonya and Nina for a while.

In four days' time he had to send off Misha. He wondered where the transplant heart had come from.

After sitting for half an hour, he went and strolled as far as the boat station, then back to the Metro and over into the second half of Hydropark, which also had its scattered groups of summer cafés. Here there were fewer people. He went as far as the bridge over the creek, beyond which there was nothing but beaches and sports grounds, then turned back. At a café still some distance from the Metro station, he sat down, ordered a Pepsi and again surveyed the scene.

They must be somewhere there, he told himself, taking in the faces, sizes and shapes of those sitting at dozens of tables.

His attention was caught by a little girl playing on the grass beside a path with wooden seats at set distances from each other, perhaps 150 metres away. On the seat nearest her, two figures were sitting, of whom he could see only the backs of their heads.

Leaving his Pepsi, he set off along the grass strip between two paths. Twenty or thirty metres from the little girl, he was no longer in any doubt – it was Sonya, either looking for something in the grass or studying it.

He stopped, and returning to the café, followed a path to the toilet from where he would be able to see who was sitting on the seat.

Outside the toilet he stopped and looked back, lifting his sunglasses to get a clearer view.

Nina sat quietly chatting with Baggy Football Jersey. Or more exactly, he was doing all the talking while she listened, nodding occasionally.

So as not to make himself conspicuous, he went into the

toilet, and when he came out set off back to the café.

He stole a glance in their direction as he went. Now *she* was talking and Baggy Football Jersey was listening.

Suddenly he felt a fool. It was not just that shadowing was deprived of its interest, but that suddenly the whole impetus of events seemed horribly banal. The fellow was obviously smitten, and making up to her. But seeing her always with a little girl and thinking her married, he was trying to get things straight and estimate his chances. To which end, pretending to be an old friend of her husband's was a sound tactic.

So what? he thought, climbing the steps to the Metro platform. Best of luck, Fat Man!

He returned to the flat well before Nina and Sonya.

"Had a good walk?" he asked.

"Lovely," said Nina, putting on the kettle. "Such weather! And you've been sitting indoors!"

"Still, the day after tomorrow we're going into the country. I'll get my air then."

"Day after tomorrow?"

"To view the dacha."

"Of course!" She waved a hand. "I'd forgotten. Like some tea?"

"I would. – See any old friends of mine today?"

"The same one again," she answered evenly with a shrug of her shoulders. "Kolya . . . Kept on about himself. How he'd wanted to be a writer even as a child, then had devoted himself to journalism . . . How his marriage had gone wrong."

"But no more questions about me?"

"No, but he was very insistent I should give him a photo of you. So he could see how you'd changed over the years. Promised us Italian ice-creams in return."

"Is he off his head?" he said, more to himself than to Nina. "What does he want my photo for?"

Again she shrugged.

"Did you arrange to meet?" he asked, giving her a searching look.

"No, but I did say I might go to Hydropark tomorrow."

"Right," he said coldly. "I'll give you a photo."

Nina looked up in surprise.

"What's wrong?" she asked in an injured voice. "Am I supposed to avoid old friends of yours?"

He went out of the kitchen, saying nothing, and made his way past Sonya playing on the living room floor with her plastic Barbie house. Shutting the bedroom door behind him, he pulled out an old portfolio from the cupboard of the bedside table and shook a bundle of photographs onto the carpet. Sorting through them, he put aside one showing him with Nika, a previous girlfriend. Replacing the rest, he took some scissors and trimmed away Nika. Standing in front of the mirror, he compared himself with the photo. Something had changed, but it was an elusive, inexplicable something. The photo had been taken four years before, in Kreshchatik Street, by a street photographer.

"Here," he said, returning to the kitchen and handing Nina the trimmed snapshot.

She looked at him questioningly.

"Take it. For next time he asks," he added, trying to put a little warmth into his voice. "And say hello from me!"

Nina looked at it with interest, and took it to the corridor where her handbag hung on a hook.

74

The next morning, as soon as Nina and Sonya had gone, Viktor fetched down the black shopping bag from the top of the wardrobe and took out the still gift-wrapped automatic. The cold, heavy metal seemed to sear his skin. Closing his hand around the grooved butt, he took aim at himself in the wardrobe mirror.

Suddenly he remembered how Misha would sometimes stand before this big mirror gazing fixedly at his reflection. Why? Was it out of loneliness? The impossibility of finding himself a mate?

He lowered his arm, feeling a disagreeable sensation in his palm, as if from the chemical reaction of two incompatible elements. Dropping the gun to the carpet, he inspected his hand. The palm was surprisingly white, as though deprived of blood by the coldness and weight of the metal.

With a sigh he stooped, picked up the gun, and thrust it into a pocket of his jeans. Another look in the mirror showed the protruding black butt and the clear outline of the weapon.

Opening the wardrobe, he found an old blue anorak with a hood, put it on and took another look in the mirror. Fine! Except that the sun on the carpet suggested the garment to be unsuited to a promise of summer warmth.

Zipping up his anorak, he left the flat.

Again Hydropark was crowded.

It's Saturday, he thought, sitting at a table of one of the pavement cafés.

Looking around, he was comforted to see others not dressed for the weather. Common or garden idiots. They couldn't all be concealing weapons! One man was wearing something like a nylon fur jacket. He was, it was true, much older than Viktor, and age may have been part of the trouble.

"Coffee and a cognac," he told the waiter standing stiffly to attention before him.

The little table-and-kiosk-filled square outside the Metro was suddenly thrown into shadow. Viktor was glad of the cloud. The weather was adapting itself to his dress.

Waiting for his coffee and cognac, he took a closer look around. No sign of Nina and Sonya, but knowing them to be somewhere about, he wasn't worried.

A quarter of an hour later he walked along between the tennis courts to the ruins of the Okhotnik Restaurant and back. After which he went under the bridge to the other side of Hydropark, to walk past the seats where Nina and the unaccountably nosy Kolya had sat the day before.

So what? he thought, still looking. He would very soon know why Kolya was interested in him and his photograph.

As the path became a track, Viktor turned back and made for the little bridge over the channel. He stopped in the middle and leant over the balustrade. Overhanging the channel somewhat gloomily on his right, was the Mlyn Restaurant. People were seated at tables on the spacious balcony, but those he sought were not among them. Parked below was a long silvery Lincoln, just like the late Misha-non-penguin's.

The sun reappeared, turning a black-and-white scene into colour. The waters danced and played, shot through with an emerald sparkle. The white concrete of the balustrade, now yellow, was not only rough to the touch, but warm from a kind of inner glow.

Heading back towards the open-air cafés he stopped dead,

having spotted Nina and Sonya. They were alone. In front of Sonya was a tall glass containing three different-coloured balls of ice-cream. Nina was drinking coffee.

Where, he wondered, looking around, was nosy Fat Man?

Selecting a table some distance away from them, he ordered coffee.

They were chatting, and every now and then Nina turned and looked in the direction of the Metro exit.

Some 15 minutes passed. Viktor finished his coffee and sat on, lost in untimely memories.

When he looked again they were a threesome. Fat Man had arrived, and the waitress was bringing coffee.

Viktor watched. Sonya sat saying nothing, while Nina talked to Fat Man. He was smiling broadly, his moon-face growing still rounder. From a pocket of his white summer jacket he produced a bar of chocolate, which he offered to Nina. She set about unwrapping it. It was, Viktor could see, stuck to the silver paper, having melted. Nina licked some of it off and passed the silver wrapping to Fat Man.

Disgusted, Viktor turned away, feeling a stab of pain in his neck from the effort of keeping watch. After massaging it a bit he looked back.

Fat Man seemed to be inviting them somewhere. He had got up and was standing at the plastic table, talking, gesticulating gently.

Nina and Sonya also got to their feet, and the trio started in Viktor's direction.

He tensed, momentarily at a loss how to conceal himself, as he sat leaning over the table, his back to the pavement where they were about to pass.

Pushing back his chair suddenly, he bent down and pretended to re-tie a shoelace.

"Do you like the circus?" asked a sugary male voice directly behind him.

"Yes, I do," said Sonya, and Viktor bent still lower.

"We've been twice already," Nina was saying, her voice growing fainter. "Once we saw the tigers, the second time . . ."

He gave them another 30 seconds before looking the way they had gone and straightening up.

They were making for the bridge over the channel, but just short of it, they turned right.

Viktor set off in hot pursuit and arrived at the bridge just in time to see them enter the Mlyn restaurant.

He went up onto the bridge, and this time stood looking the opposite way towards Vladimir Hill. After about ten minutes he turned, and there they were, on the restaurant balcony, Fat Man in conversation with the waiter, Nina with Sonya.

He didn't see the hand-over of the photograph, but the bottle of champagne on their balcony table infuriated him even more than their sharing melted chocolate. His fury could not have been greater if he had actually seen the photograph pass into Fat Man's hands. Unlike the champagne and the chocolate, that was something he had anticipated.

The sun continued to shine, and Viktor was hot in his anorak, the discomfort of this only adding to his fury. He was now leaning over the balustrade, watching Sonya again. She was eating ice-cream while Nina and Fat Man did the same between sips of champagne.

When they emerged an hour later, Viktor set off behind them, staying well back. At the Metro entrance under the bridge they stopped, and he stopped too, keeping his distance.

Fat Man was taking his leave in rather modest fashion, without so much as a peck on the cheek for Nina. Viktor watched the ceremony with a malicious sense of irony, until Fat Man disappeared into the Metro, and Nina and Sonya made for the other side of Hydropark.

Viktor set off quickly after Fat Man, and spotting him on the platform, dodged behind a pillar.

They boarded a city train, entering the carriage by adjacent doors, and now he got a good look at Fat Man, standing sideways on to him reading one of the dozens of adverts stuck to the inside of the windows.

It was the first time he had seen him close to. He was wearing wide mouse-coloured canvas trousers and a white summer jacket over a dark-orange football jersey.

His appearance said nothing – he could have been anybody or nobody, so total was the lack of detail suggestive of either character or employment.

At Central Station he alighted. So did Viktor, and suddenly finding himself close behind Fat Man, he dropped back until the latter set foot on the escalator; then, with other passengers between them, Viktor did the same, keeping him in sight.

They crossed the platform of Central Station and came out by way of the underpass at the top of Uritsky Street. In company with Fat Man, Viktor waited for a tram, and travelled two stops, getting off when he did.

Fat Man looked once in his direction, but that was all. Either he didn't know Viktor by sight, or he wasn't particularly observant.

The street was fairly deserted and Viktor hung back at the tram stop. He watched Fat Man walk up a path beside a car park towards a multi-storey building somewhat removed from the road.

Viktor followed slowly along the same path, and seeing Fat Man heading for the entrance to the building, he halted and waited for him to go in.

In a flash he, too, was at the entrance, standing at the open door, listening, and noticing out of the corner of his eye the familiar blue Moskvich estate parked outside.

The entrance hall was empty and silent but for the hum of a lift. The service lift door was open, but above the closed door of the passenger lift a succession of tiny bulbs was lighting its unhurried upward progress. At last the hum ceased, and the bulb by 13 went out.

Entering the service lift, Viktor pressed the button for Floor 13.

Emerging on Floor 13, he was confronted by a graffiti-scrawled wall and abandoned cardboard boxes.

The landing door led into a long dark corridor smelling of dog.

He listened at doors as he passed. From one came the shrill barking of a wretched dog. At one end of the long corridor there was a window, but the light from it penetrated scarcely half way to the lift exit.

At the dark end of the corridor, he stopped and listened again. Outside one door stood a child's bicycle. Outside another, opposite, chained and padlocked to a pipe conveying water or gas to all floors, was a car tyre cover. He went and stood close to the door. Faint sounds were audible, a door creaked, a lavatory flushed.

His eyes having by now accustomed themselves to the semi-darkness, he took in the brown leatherette upholstery of the door and the black doorbell button. He had already wiped his

214

feet on the crumpled cloth in front of the door, but seized by a familiar, partly understandable fit of indecision, he stood wondering whether it was worth trying to discover the reason for Fat Man's curiosity. What if he wouldn't say?

He felt for the gun, still heavy on his thigh, and was reassured, having made certain it was still there.

We're all entitled to satisfy our curiosity, he thought. And now it's my turn.

He gave the black button a determined press, and four bars of *Moscow Nights* resulted.

Shuffling steps came to the door.

"Who's there?" wheezed a man's voice.

"A neighbour."

The lock clicked, the door opened just a little, and a flabby man of about 50 in pyjama trousers and singlet looked out.

For a moment Viktor stood staring into a round, unshaven face.

"What do you want?" the man asked.

Barging him aside, Viktor found himself in the corridor. He quickly took in the layout, ignoring the stupefied master of the house, and there, peering out of the open bathroom door, was Fat Man.

"Who do you want?" Pyjama Trousers managed to get out.

"Him!" said Viktor, pointing.

Pyjama Trousers followed his gaze.

"Kolya?" he asked, aghast.

Kolya, clearly startled, shrugged.

"Who are you?" he asked slowly.

Viktor shook his head, surprised.

"What a question to ask!" he said.

He motioned Fat Man in the direction of the kitchen.

215

Fat Man led, Viktor followed.

"What do you want?" Fat Man asked, standing with his back to the window.

"To find out why you need my photo and take such an interest in my life."

Comprehension dawned on Fat Man's face. Staring thoughtfully at his uninvited visitor, he reached slowly into an inner pocket of his white summer jacket, produced the photo, and looked at it and at Viktor.

Viktor was emboldened by his obvious dismay.

"I'm listening!" he said, a note of menace in his voice.

Fat Man said nothing.

Slowly unzipping his anorak, Viktor produced the automatic, and without actually threatening him, let him get the message.

Fat Man moistened his lips as if they were suddenly dry.

"I can't tell you," he said in a trembling voice.

At the sound of shuffling steps, Viktor swung round, and looking into another frightened face, raised the automatic.

"Get lost," he said, and Pyjama Trousers retreated into the corridor.

"Well?" Viktor glared, his patience wearing thin.

"I was promised work . . ." began Fat Man. "This was my first assignment."

"What sort of work?"

"With a newspaper . . . Sort of interviews . . ." His voice trembled. "I worked in a different section . . . This was better paid."

Sort of interviews? Was that what *he* had been writing all these months? Was Fat Man his replacement?

That bleak conjecture had a numbing effect, and an old

suppressed fear reared its head, striving to take possession of his thoughts and feelings.

"What's the photo for?" Viktor asked icily.

"It wasn't essential. It was just that having learnt so much about you, I wanted to see your face."

"My face . . . What's my face got to do with you? When I wrote *sort of interviews*, faces were of no interest to me. Show me what you've written!"

Fat Man didn't budge.

"I can't. If they find out –"

"They won't!"

Fat Man marched along the corridor to a bedroom where there was a desk in front of the window with a typewriter on it. To left and right of the machine were orderly piles of paper – indeed, the room itself was excessively tidy. But the air was oppressive and stuffy, as though breathed for months without ventilation.

Fat Man went over to the desk, closely followed by Viktor.

His hands were shaking. He turned and faced his visitor.

"Let's have it!" urged Viktor.

With a heavy sigh Fat Man extracted a sheet from a green folder.

The brief but eventful life of Viktor Zolotaryov would suffice for a substantial trilogy, such as, it must be supposed, will in due course be written. Meanwhile, by way of a sad note to that future trilogy, it is his obituary that must be written.

Had he stuck to literature or journalism, he could safely have been described as an author *manqué*. But while clearly lacking purely literary talent, he possessed a manifest surplus of talent for the invention of subjects and plots. He did not go the way of more senior authors *manqués* – into quiet politics and a peaceful doze sitting as a deputy. But revealing his real interest to be for politics, he discovered a rather unexpected application for his talents.

A great deal concerning his life remains at present a mystery. And that includes the exact moment of his association with State Security Group A. But following this association, Viktor Zolotaryov became obsessed with a need to *cleanse* society. And already it is possible to identify some results of his abruptly curtailed politico-literary activity: 118 killings or deaths under suspicious circumstances, of persons, all, to use a Western term, of VIP calibre – from State Deputies to Ministers and factory managers – all persons of not-unclouded antecedents, on whom Group A had opened files. The impossibility – by virtue of Deputy immunity or judicial corruptibility – of bringing these persons to book, was evidently what, in the final analysis, led Group A agents to employ Viktor Zolotaryov. His *obituaries of the still living* became, uniquely, indents for future death, each supplying *per se* ample cause.

His appointment – through the good offices of our late Assistant Arts Editor – to be a freelance correspondent of this paper, proved ideal cover.

Much remains to be discovered, but already it can be stated that he not only made future death a basis for social justice, but even determined the date and manner of death – sometimes an unduly cruel one. Ballistic examination of the Stechkin automatic with which he shot himself, permits the supposition that he had personally taken part in at least one *social cleansing* operation, Deputy Yakornitsky having been killed with this weapon and hurled from a sixth storey.

The personal life of Viktor Zolotaryov was also more literary invention than real, the sole creature to which he showed genuine attachment being a penguin. So highly did he value his penguin, that on its falling seriously ill, he arranged for the transplant of a child's heart, buying it, literally, from the parents of a boy fatally injured in a motor accident, regardless of the ethical and moral questions involved.

Another mystery is that of his link with bosses of the criminal world, among whom he was known as *The Penguin*. A striking feature is the frequency with which he attended the funerals of persons he had assisted in killing, completing as it were, an original cycle: from file of future departed, to participation, with friends and relatives, in the departed's wake.

Now that the *social cleansing* operation he conceived and carried through has reached the public domain, there is hope that the full details will become known. A Committee of Deputies is already conducting an inquiry. The Head of Group A has been relieved of his duties, and while his name, like that of his successor, is kept secret, there are grounds for believing that nothing similar will recur, and that no organ of State Security will in future abrogate to itself the right to sit in judgement on anyone, criminals outside the law included.

Viktor Zolotaryov's contribution to the literature of

our young country is nil, but his contribution to the political history of Ukraine may well become a subject of research not only by a Committee of Deputies, but by his fellow writers also. And who knows, a novel on that theme may enjoy a longer and more successful life than that of Viktor Zolotaryov.

He looked up at Fat Man, and Fat Man looked at him, awaiting his judgement.

Viktor deposited the sheet of paper on the table without a word, oppressed by a sudden heavy burden.

He remembered the Chief's *When you do know what's what, it will mean there no longer is any real point to your work or to your continuing existence.*

The weight in his right hand brought his thoughts back to the automatic, which he now knew to be a Stechkin.

Fat Man was watching closely, his round face gradually losing its look of fear, his lips moving as if framing thoughts.

"Well?" he ventured at last, faced with a softened, no longer aggressive Viktor.

Viktor looked wearily at him. "Well, what?"

"Well, what I've written . . ."

"Dry as dust . . . lousy opening . . . newspapery . . . *here!*" He held out the gun to the flabbergasted Fat Man. "Something to remember me by."

Eyes riveted on Viktor, Fat Man held out both hands for it.

Viktor's right hand was its unencumbered self again. Giving Fat Man the gun was like throwing off an illness. Turning silently on his heel, he walked out of the flat.

75

Viktor sat until midnight with hundreds of passengers in the waiting hall at the Central Station, listening to muffled and unintelligible arrival and departure announcements.

He sat in his anorak, and froze.

He no longer felt afraid. It was not that he was resigned or had given up. After the shock of reading his own *obelisk*, the noise of the busy station resuscitated him. All right, his end was imminent and obvious: the same people who had created him in the image of a future *notable*, had already determined what that end should be – suicide – and when it should be. Having no idea who they were, he should have been in mortal fear of anyone sitting or passing near. But there was no point. Fear was for those who still had a chance of staying alive. Sitting there at the station, he could see no such chance, though he would have liked to prolong his life, if only by a day or two.

At the same time he felt hurt that his own *obelisk* should be the product of so obviously untalented a hand.

He, he thought, would have made a better job of it, but immediately rejected the idea as crass and obscene.

And why no mention of Nina and Sonya? Why just Misha? Someone must have known him better than he knew himself. It was obvious, too, that those who had compiled the file were better informed than he. They had even known, as he had not, the source of the donor heart.

The train arriving at Track 9 is the train from Lvov for Moscow, declared an indistinct tinny voice, and the women sitting around him sprang up, shouldering heavy sacks and lifting enormous shopping bags.

He felt ill at ease. Firstly, because he was in their way, and secondly, because when they had gone, the whole row would be empty. He got up too, and made for the station exit.

It was about one when he arrived back at the flat. He shut the door quietly behind him and took off his shoes.

Nina and Sonya were asleep.

Without turning on the light, he sat down at the kitchen table, and looked out at the windows of the block opposite. Only one was lit, on the first floor, over the entrance, which was, he thought, where the caretaker woman lived.

In a far corner of the window ledge he noticed a mayonnaise pot with a candle. It stirred a memory. Fetching matches from the stove, he put the pot on the table and lit the candle.

The nervy flame cast trembling shadows on the kitchen walls. For a while he gazed, fascinated, then, taking pen and paper, wrote:

> Dear Nina,
> In a bag on top of the wardrobe is Sonya's money.
> Look after her. Got to go away for a bit. Back when the
> dust settles . . .

The last sentence wrote itself, and he was about to underline it, but stopped and simply read it over several times. It had a soothing ring.

> All the best, – Viktor.

he added, pushed the note from him, and sat for a long while contemplating the candle flame.

The dark-green urn with lid still stood on the window ledge, its surface reflecting the gentle glow of the candle.

Style was a word beloved of bearded Lyosha. Maybe he, Viktor, should invent a style of his own. Do something new before suicide. Go where he had never been before and where no one would think of looking for him!

The candle lit a sad smile.

Quietly he went through to the bedroom and opened the wardrobe. From the pocket of his winter jacket he took his own bundle of dollars earned in conjunction with Misha. He went back to the kitchen and had another look out of the window. It would be cold, out there in the dark. Going again to the bedroom, he came back with a sweater, which he put on under his anorak. And shoving the weighty bundle of dollars into his pocket, he left the flat.

76

For $10 the taxi driver drove him to the door of *Casino Johnny* where his way was barred by a massive, dark-suited guard. Something about his mighty frame and aggressive manner moved Viktor to laughter. Flashing his bundle of notes and peeling one off, heedless of denomination, he stuck it in the guard's breast pocket. The guard stepped aside.

A girl cashier in a snow-white blouse with a pale-blue scarf around her neck dozed behind her window. For a night-spot it was too quiet. He looked around, puzzled, having imagined something very different.

He tapped on the glass. The girl woke, and looked in surprise at his anorak.

He proffered $100, and was handed a number of different-coloured plastic counters.

"This your first time here?" she asked, seeing his doubtful response. "They're instead of money. For use in the bar, and for placing bets."

He looked around, unsure where to go.

"That way," she prompted, pointing to a heavy green curtain.

It was another world he found himself in, more like what he had imagined, except that it was still too quiet. There were, by his estimate, no more than seven people in the whole place. A man was playing alone against the croupier at one of the roulette tables; at another, three men were playing. Two more were playing poker. There was soft music, and from a corridor, neon-signed *Bar*, a girl came in with a glass of wine.

Viktor went over to the table at which the lone man was playing. He might have been Japanese or Korean, and was placing his stakes in a subdued, embittered sort of way.

Viktor sat beside him, watched what he did, then made his first bet.

The tiny ball sped around, stopped, and the croupier slid some counters towards him.

He had won!

Roulette was something he had seen only at the cinema, and this was like a film he had never seen before. With sudden abandon, he placed all his counters on red, and won again, watched with evident mistrust by the Japanese-Korean.

Placing all his counters on even, Viktor won again.

This was tedious. Shoving the counters into a pocket of his

anorak, he went to the bar, ordered a large cognac, and as change for his counter, got back three of a different colour.

Toy money, toy prices, toy people – this was a Children's World indeed . . .

Returning, glass in hand to the tables, he sat down at the same one, staked a fistful of counters, and won again.

Beginner's luck, he decided.

The Japanese-Korean took himself off, and Viktor played on alone. Played and won. The plastic results of which began to weigh down both pockets.

"Look," he said, addressing the croupier, an elegant young man in white shirt and bow tie, "what do I do with these counters?"

"Change them back into dollars," was the answer.

Viktor nodded, and went on winning.

Then back to the bar. After which, the restaurant. A dumpy woman of no age or figure. A hotel room . . . All he could remember was the strength of her arms.

Next morning, head buzzing, Viktor woke alone. He got up and looked out of the window at the familiar square with its little market.

He wasn't going anywhere, he decided. He still had money that he wouldn't be needing . . .

Struck by sudden doubt, he took his anorak off the chair and felt in the pockets. To his surprise, the bundle of dollars and mass of counters were still there.

When he had washed and dressed he went down to the restaurant, and for a few counters had an excellent meal and more to drink. Back in his room, he slept until evening, then went down again, this time to the casino.

His second night was even more successful than the first. He went on winning, not caring what might happen to him. He realized subconsciously that to go on winning was bad. At the same time this seemed strange, since people played to win.

After a good spell in the bar, he proceeded to the cashier's desk. There was no one there, but another elegant young man of about 17, also in white shirt and bow tie, appeared, having evidently noticed him.

Viktor started shedding counters from the pockets of his anorak onto the shelf in front of the window.

Catching a flash of alarm in the young man's eyes, he stopped and stared.

The young man gave a barely perceptible shake of the head.

"You oughtn't to cash all that lot in," he whispered, "you'll never get away from here."

"So what do I do?" asked Viktor, at something of a loss.

"Play until morning, then phone some friends to meet you at the door."

"That's the local rule, is it?" Viktor said, drunkenly surprised.

"No," said the young man. "We play by the book, unlike most." He nodded towards the green curtain through which Viktor had entered the night before.

Leaving his counters at the window, Viktor went and looked through the curtain. In the hotel foyer, not five metres away, four thugs stood chatting. One gave him a cheery wink.

Gathering up his counters, Viktor played on, and towards dawn fell asleep on a comfortable black leather settee in the bar.

At about nine he was woken by someone who rummaged in his pockets for his key on its hefty hotel pear, and conducted him to his room.

For his third night at the tables he felt as if his powers were deserting him. He had a mist before his eyes and could hardly see where he was placing his counters. But he still kept winning, and in the end grew apprehensive, under the cold, lifeless gaze of the nattily dressed, neatly cropped croupiers and house security guards.

Towards morning one of them came over to him.

"Like us to see you home?" he asked, his face frozen in a waxen smile.

"*Home?*" For Viktor it was a word of menace.

"Don't worry, we'd drive you in the limo – with an escort, if you like. You could cash your chips, or leave them and come back."

"What's the date?" he asked suddenly.

"Ninth of May," replied Waxen Smile.

"And the time?"

"7.30."

Viktor tried to think. The 9th of May. Not just former Victory Day, but the day of Misha's flight . . . Only not now. Misha was at the Theophania Clinic, which was where they would be waiting, eager to close Viktor's dead hand around the Stechkin automatic.

"Could you, in an hour's time, take me to the aircraft factory?" he asked after a moment's hesitation.

They looked at him amazed.

"Certainly," said Waxen Smile. "With escort?"

Viktor nodded.

The man withdrew.

The limousine was enormous. He had never seen such a vehicle. It was like sitting in a room. The escort served him with a gin and tonic from a small refrigerator.

They drove along Victory Avenue, and through the tinted glass

Viktor could see people stopping to watch the limo pass.

He smiled contentedly, sipping another gin and tonic. He was still drunk. Pulling out a fistful of chips, he offered them to the escort. The latter accepted with thanks.

They pulled up at the factory gate and the escort enquired, "Where now?"

"Ask Valentin Ivanovich of the Antarctic Committee to meet me here."

The escort got out, and Viktor watched him walk calmly through the checkpoint and disappear inside the building. No one stopped him.

Five minutes later he returned.

"He's waiting," he said, indicating the checkpoint.

"You can go," said Viktor, getting out.

Valentin Ivanovich looked thoroughly alarmed, but seeing Viktor, heaved a sigh of relief.

"Phew! I didn't know it was you," he said. "Where's the penguin?"

"The penguin," said Viktor bleakly, "is me."

Valentin Ivanovich nodded thoughtfully.

"Let's go," he said. "We're loading."

December 1995 – February 1996